D1557503

VICTORIA

VICTORIA

by
Silvana Goldemberg

Translated from the Spanish
by Emilie Smith

VANCOUVER   LONDON

Distribution and representation in Canada by
Fitzhenry & Whiteside • www.fitzhenry.ca

Distribution and representation in the UK by
Turnaround • www.turnaround-uk.com

Published in Canada in October 2013
Published in the UK and the US in 2014

Text © 2013 by Silvana Goldemberg
English translation © Emilie Smith
Cover photography: background © www.danheller.com
image of girl © Rami Katz
Translation by Emilie Smith
Cover and book design by Jacqueline Wang

Mixed Sources

Cert no. SW-COC-001271
© 1996 FSC

FSC

Inside pages printed on FSC certified paper using vegetable-based inks.

Manufactured by Sunrise Printing
Manufactured in Vancouver, BC, Canada in October 2013

2 4 6 8 10 9 7 5 3 1

Cataloguing-in-Publication Data for this book
is available from The British Library.

Library and Archives Canada Cataloguing in Publication

Goldemberg, Silvana, 1963-, author
Victoria / Silvana Goldemberg ; Emilie Smith (translator).

Originally written in Spanish under the same title.
ISBN 978-1-896580-95-1 (pbk.)

I. Smith, Emilie, 1963-, translator II. Title.

PS8613.O438V5313 2013   jC863'.7   C2013-902658-4

*Tradewind Books wishes to thank
Anouk Moser, Rosemary Hall, Arushi Raina,
Elsa Delacretaz and Lynda Tierney
for their editorial help with this project.*

*Tradewind Books thanks the Governments of Canada and British Columbia for
the financial support they have extended through the Canada Book Fund, Livres
Canada Books, the Canada Council for the Arts, the British Columbia Arts
Council and the British Columbia Book Publishing Tax Credit program.*

**Canada Council
for the Arts**

**Conseil des Arts
du Canada**

BRITISH COLUMBIA
ARTS COUNCIL
Supported by the Province of British Columbia

Canadä

LIVRES CANADA BOOKS

"If I were hungry and destitute,
I would not ask for a loaf of bread,
I would ask for half a loaf and a book . . .
Enjoy the fruit of the human spirit—
not to do so is to be a slave."
Federico García Lorca, Granada, 1929

Acknowledgements

*I want to thank the following people for their kindness
in answering my inquiries: Susana Goldemberg,
Adrián Goldemberg, Dr. Ruth Faifman, Dr. Alberto
Kaplan, Claudia Abramzon, Susana Bloj, Luciana
Maffioly, Livio Incatasciato, Andy and Martín
Goldemberg, Gonzalo and Federico Rochlin, Caroline
Adderson, Irene N. Watts, Cindy Heinrichs, Alison
Acheson, Cathy Moss, Anna Archer, Rhea Tregebov,
Ingrid Putkonen, María Carbonetti , Maia and
Muriel Faifman; Michael Katz for helping Victoria's
voice be heard; Mary Ann Thompson for her editing
work and support. And to all of my family and friends
who allowed me to find, through the creation of this
book, the convergence between work and pleasure.*

For the children who suffer from violence and poverty.
For the justice and dignity they deserve.

Any similarity between fiction and reality has more to
do with coexistence than coincidence.

Silvana Goldemberg

CHAPTER ONE

Moonlight shines on the photo taped to the wall beside her pillow. Lying in bed, Victoria gazes at the happy scene—she and her mother are smiling for the camera, their long brown hair done up with flowers for her mother's birthday.

I miss you so much, Mamá. I don't want to turn fifteen without you. I can't. And the twins—poor little ones. Every day they ask for you.

Victoria imagines her mother answering, her voice full of love. "Don't worry, *m'hija*. Everything will be okay."

When will everything be okay, Mamá?

Victoria tosses and turns. She closes her eyes, but cannot sleep. She wishes that her mother were still alive, and she and her brothers were back home in their old neighbourhood on the other side of Paraná.

I'm still here in Betina's room.

The wall is covered with posters of *cumbia* singers. An

oval mirror with a red plastic frame hangs above her cousin's empty bed. *She's probably at a boyfriend's.*

Victoria's twin brothers are asleep on a third bed. It is jammed into the small room against a huge old wardrobe, which holds their few belongings.

A snore rumbles from the next room. The slow rhythmic sound comforts Victoria. *Doña Norma is much nicer than Aunt Marta. But she's so old.*

Hours seem to pass.

Victoria wonders if the twins are stirring. She gets up to check on them. They're sleeping deeply. *No nightmares so far.* Victoria watches them dream. They lie back-to-back with their feet sticking out from underneath the quilt. Damian sucks his thumb, while Martin twists his hair.

On the other side of the small house, Aunt Marta and her boyfriend, Juan, argue. Martin whimpers and turns over before settling again.

Victoria returns to her bed and covers her ears. She thinks of her mother tucking her in while humming the tango.

> *Sleep, mi amor.*
> *The angels will watch over you.*
> *Dream, mi amor.*
> *If tomorrow you don't find me*
> *with you when you awake,*
> *look to the heavens, beloved.*
> *That's where I will be . . .*

Victoria buries her head in the pillow and cries silently.

The angry voices grow louder.

"I'm sick to death of this place," Juan says. "If you don't send those kids to an orphanage, I'll leave for good!"

I wish he really would leave instead of always pretending he will.

A truck backfires by Victoria's window, drowning Juan's voice out for a moment, and then his ranting is back. "And the old lady—always bothering us. And her snoring! It drives me crazy. She should go live with her son in Buenos Aires."

"*Idiota*, Doña Norma owns the house," Marta shouts. "And I don't see *you* bringing in any money. Maybe you should go and look for work."

Glass shatters on the street. Someone screams. Victoria scrambles to the window.

Three boys are on top of Danny, the grocer's son, pounding him. A broken bottle lies on the ground a few feet away. "You'd better get the money, *hijo de puta*!"

One of the boys looks up at Victoria's window. The scar on his forehead is bright red in the moonlight. Victoria draws back into the room. *I hope he didn't see me.*

After a long moment, Victoria peeks out from behind the curtain again. The boys are jumping into the back of a rusty pick-up truck. Danny is painfully making his way to the grocery.

As the truck speeds off, the boy with the red scar shouts, "You better have the money tomorrow, Danny!"

Poor Danny . . .

"Go to hell!" Marta yells.

A violent slam shakes the house, and Juan barrels down the street.

He looks drunk.

She pulls the curtain shut—she doesn't want Juan to see her at the window.

There is a forlorn cry inside the room, followed by a second. The twins are awake.

"Come on, get up! Move your lazy butt!" Aunt Marta's voice wakes Victoria. "There's a mountain of ironing to do, and you've got to take the skirts to Mrs. Meitry and get the medicine for Doña Norma."

Victoria drags herself up, tired from lack of sleep. The twins' bed is empty. She hears a shout and a laugh—they are playing outside with the kids next door. *It's good they have new friends and can have some fun.*

This morning will be no different than any other since she and her brothers came to stay with their aunt: Victoria will clean the house, iron clothes, deliver them to clients and make lunch. *Another "wonderful" day.*

She is washing the breakfast dishes when her aunt comes

in to boil water for *mate* to drink while she sews.

Victoria takes a deep breath. "*Tía*, since the twins are going to start school, I was thinking that I . . . "

"Oh, so you've been thinking, have you?" her aunt snaps.

"Yes," Victoria says. Now that she's started, she may as well continue. "It's just that . . . I'd like to go back to school."

"Stop bothering me with your nonsense."

"Please, Tía. My mother . . . "

"Don't even think about it." Her aunt is furious. "You have too much to do around here. I can't slave away all day so the *princesa* can live in luxury."

But Victoria has dreams. "I'd still be able to help out. School is only a few hours a day."

"I said no. Now peel those potatoes for lunch!" Kettle in hand, her aunt storms out of the kitchen, leaving a trail of steam behind her.

"Someday I want to be a teacher," Victoria says. But nobody hears her.

She peels the potatoes. *Aunt Marta doesn't care about me. She just wants me to work for her. Mamá would want me to go to school.*

"What are you cooking up, *cosita*?"

Victoria freezes. It's Juan. He puts a hand on her waist and leans into her, his breath stinking of the cheap nasty wine he drinks.

She ducks away and shoves him. Juan staggers and tries to

stay upright. Victoria shows him the peeling knife and yells, "Keep your hands off me!"

"Hey, *linda*, don't get upset about nothing." Juan smiles as he speaks, showing his yellow teeth. His eyes are bloodshot.

Why does Aunt Marta stay with this man?

Juan moves toward her.

"Get away from me, disgusting pig! Don't ever touch me again!" Victoria shouts. She runs to Betina's bedroom and slams the door shut.

"VICTORIAAA!" HER AUNT SHOUTS. "GET BACK TO THE kitchen and finish cooking lunch. Stop wasting time!"

Why doesn't she ever believe me when I tell her about Juan? Can't she see for herself what he's up to?

"VICTORIAAA! What are you doing? Get out of your room and stop sulking!"

Victoria looks at her mother's photo. *She was so kind and strong for us. I have to be strong as well.*

"*Mierda*! VICTORIA!" Her aunt is shouting again, now from Doña Norma's room. "VICTORIAAA! Bring the mop. The old lady has pissed on the floor. VICTORIAAAAA! DO YOU HEAR ME?"

THAT EVENING, VICTORIA RETURNS FROM PICKING UP HER aunt's sewing. Juan's bike is crowding the narrow entry hall, so she squeezes by, careful to keep the clothes from brushing up against it. The house is quiet except for Doña Norma's snores.

As soon as Victoria enters the dining room, Juan comes in from Marta's room. "Hi, cosita!" He reeks of alcohol.

Victoria steps back in disgust and fear. "Where are the twins and Marta?"

"Who cares where the hell they are. We're okay without them," Juan says, cornering her against the wall.

"Leave me alone." Victoria shoves the sewing at him and spins away. But Juan lunges at her, grabs her arms and presses against her. His smell nauseates her. In horror, she punches and kicks at him; but the more she struggles, the more violent he becomes.

Finally, Victoria sinks her teeth into his arm, biting hard. Juan yells and slaps her sharply across her face. Reflexively, she knees him, and Juan doubles over and falls down.

"Go to hell, hijo de puta!" Victoria says, and she bolts into the street where she can choose her own misery.

CHAPTER TWO

VICTORIA DARTS INTO AN ALLEY AND SKIDS TO A STOP. Two guys are dragging a third. One is holding a gun. She recognizes him. *The one with the scar.*

Victoria quickly slips behind a broken garden fence into a yard and crouches down. Her heart pounds so strongly she's afraid it will jump out of her chest.

"No . . . please . . . no!" someone shouts.

It's Danny.

Silence follows his plea. Victoria is desperate with fear. She looks at the house across the yard. It's dark. She gets up, determined to seek help.

A muffled gunshot rings out.

A light snaps on from a window across the alley, illuminating Danny's thin body lying in the dirt. Victoria claps her hand over her mouth to stop herself from screaming.

Footsteps.

The boys are fleeing. The smaller one stops and stares at Victoria. He's wide-eyed, frightened.

"Quick!" hisses the one with the scar. He sees Victoria, scowls ferociously and slows.

Shouts, and the two boys vanish into the dark alleyways.

Two women burst out of a door and run over to Danny. "*Jesús María*, the kid's dead!"

Victoria gets up and dashes between the houses. She races down narrow streets and keeps running until her chest aches. Finally she reaches Urquiza Park and stops in front of the statue of an Indian girl holding an arrow. A dizzy spell knocks her off balance and she crouches down, gasping for breath.

Poor Danny. He was so kind. Sometimes he gave her leftover vegetables at the end of the day to give to her aunt.

Tears run down her cheeks. She stumbles over to a water fountain by the ice cream stand and splashes her face. She drinks so quickly that she chokes.

"Hey, *che*! That's only for customers," one of the men who works there shouts.

"Sorry," Victoria says, moving to a nearby wooden bench. She sits down, clutching the edge of the seat and tries to calm herself.

A group of boys approaches her. "What are you doing here? This is our spot!" the tallest one shouts.

"I just needed to rest a bit," Victoria says, but she gets up and walks away unsteadily.

"That's right, go home to your mommy," the boy sneers.

The other boys laugh and high-five him. He lights up a cigarette.

VICTORIA WEAVES HER WAY DOWN MORE STREETS, TRYING to be invisible. A hand grabs her shoulder from behind. She freezes.

"Give us your money!" a voice hisses.

Victoria doesn't answer.

She is spun roughly around. A different group of boys is threatening her.

"Give us your money or you'll regret it." The boy is stocky, and he has tattoos all over his arms.

"I don't have any money," Victoria says.

"Let's see if this loosens up your pocket," the tattooed boy says, punching her in the stomach.

"I've got nothing. Please leave me alone!"

The boy pushes Victoria away in disgust, and she falls, her frail body slapping hard against the pavement.

Everything hurts, inside and out. It is too much. Everything that has happened to her; everything she has lost.

Just then a shout rings out from the shadows. "Hey! Leave her alone!" A skinny old man is walking toward them. "Get them, Brownie!"

A large brown dog runs up and leaps at the boys, barking and snarling. They run off, cursing.

"Come back, Brownie. Here, boy!" the old man says, coming up to Victoria. "He won't hurt you."

"Thanks for helping me," she says, picking herself slowly off the ground.

"You're lucky they didn't kill you," the old man says. He is pushing a supermarket cart full of junk. He has a kind face, with twinkling grey eyes and a beard. There's a small black puppy with a white spot around his left eye trotting behind him. "I'm Pepperoni, but you can call me Pepe."

"I'm Victoria."

Pointing to the dogs, Pepe adds, "You've met Brownie, and this little one is Bite'm."

"Bite'm?" Victoria asks.

"Yep. Now I'm going to lie down. I've been hoofing it all the way from Oro Verde."

"That's really far," Victoria says, remembering bus rides there with her mother and brothers to visit her great aunt Raquel.

"It is. Look, I know a safe place to sleep, if you have nowhere else to go."

The worn-out wheels of the cart slap against the street as they walk. The dogs follow.

When they arrive at Centenario School, Pepperoni gestures for Victoria to follow him up the steps. He points to a spot near the front door. "You can sleep here." Then he pulls a thin blanket full of holes out of his cart and offers it to her.

"No, thanks. I'm okay," Victoria answers. She is touched by his kindness, but the blanket smells so awful, she can't bear to take it.

Pepe shrugs and wraps it around his shoulders.

Victoria sits down and leans against the wall of the school, hugging her legs. Brownie wags his tail and curls up next to her. Bite'm comes over and licks her cheek. While Victoria pets the dogs, Pepe searches through his cart, moving bottles and bags until he finds a suitable piece of cardboard.

"Here, lie down on this. It will help you stay dry."

"Sure, thank you." Victoria takes it gratefully.

Pepe takes a bottle out of his jacket pocket and drinks greedily. Finally he stops, burps, looks at Victoria, as if asking forgiveness for his lack of manners, and offers her a drink.

She shakes her head, managing a smile.

Then he takes a bruised apple out of a bag and hands it to her. "Here, che. You must be hungry."

"Thanks." Victoria takes the apple and rubs it against her shirt. It's sweet and juicy, and she savours every bite.

Bite'm licks his paw, and Brownie scratches behind his ear.

"Your cart is like a magician's hat," Victoria says, "You make things appear from it."

"Well, young lady, to avoid disappearing, you need to be a kind of magician," Pepperoni says. Lifting up the bottle, he adds, "Now let it rain!" and takes another sip.

He must have a sad story, being all alone and homeless. Victoria lies down on the cardboard and feels a chill from the cement under her. *Now I'm homeless too.* She shivers. *But I can't go back tonight. Not tomorrow. Not even the day after tomorrow.*

She covers her face with her arm to block out the cold. *I hope the twins are sleeping well. I hope they won't worry too much when they find out I'm gone.* She blows an imaginary kiss to each one. *I promise, Mamá, I promise I'll come back for them.*

CHAPTER THREE

VICTORIA SNUGGLES INTO THE BLANKET, EXPECTING THE familiar smell of her aunt's bed sheets. Instead, a nasty stench assaults her. "Yuck!"

She sits up and throws the thin blanket as far away as possible.

Pepe is asleep with his head against the wall of the school. *He must have covered me up while I slept.*

Brownie is curled up beside him, but Bite'm bounces over to her and licks her hand.

Victoria shivers with cold in the damp morning air. Her throat aches.

The school door opens, and a man in a grey uniform steps out. "Hey, Pepperoni, I haven't seen you in a while," he says.

Pepe gets up, yawning. "I've been making my rounds."

"You have to leave now. School will be starting soon." The

man smiles kindly before disappearing into the building.

"Will you stay here again tonight, Pepe?" Victoria asks hopefully.

He shakes his head. "No, I won't make it back. I'm on my way to Cerrito. Maybe in a few days." He puts his stuff into the cart. "You can keep the blanket and stay here tonight if you have nowhere else to go. Brownie! Bite'm! Let's go!"

Victoria waves goodbye, and feels a sudden pang of loneliness as Pepe walks down the street, slowly pushing his trolley. The two dogs bark and run beside him.

A faucet sticks out between some rose bushes and low palms. Victoria hurries to it and washes her hands, arms and face. Her forehead feels warm. *If only I could get my whole body under the tap and scrub myself clean.*

As she untangles her long hair with her fingers, some students on the way to school stare at her. *I'm gonna go to school too. Soon.*

One student snickers, but Victoria pays no attention to her. As she washes the blanket under the faucet, she sings one of her mother's favourite tangos:

> *When I was a child, I looked at you from a distance*
> *as one of those things that can never be reached . . .*

She wrings the blanket out, over and over, trying to squeeze out a little of her anxiety with each drop of water.

Victoria's face feels hot, and her feet are freezing. She leans up against a tree and wipes her forehead with her sleeve. A sharp pain in her stomach forces her to bend over, and she vomits a green runny fluid dotted with apple seeds. Drops of sweat cover her face. *The San Roque is near here. I'd better go there.*

It takes her more than an hour to get to San Roque, the children's hospital. She has to stop frequently as waves of nausea wash over her. When she finally gets there, the waiting room is filled with women—some of them pregnant, others carrying babies or holding the hands of small children.

Victoria joins a line at the counter. When her turn comes, a fat woman in a sky-blue smock asks, "Are you here on your own, young lady?"

"My mom dropped me off," Victoria lies. "She went to work." She swallows, and the bile burns her throat.

"Name."

"Victoria."

"Victoria what?"

"Victoria Díaz."

As the receptionist writes in the registry book, she continues, "Address?"

Victoria makes it up. "Salta . . . 627." She's afraid they'll contact her aunt.

"Okay, honey. Wait there." The woman points. "The doctor will call you when it's your turn."

Victoria squeezes onto a wooden bench between a pregnant woman and a mother with two children.

"DÍAZ? VICTORIA DÍAZ?"

Victoria wakes up with a start. She had fallen asleep, her head resting on the shoulder of an old lady. The pregnant woman and the mother are gone.

"What time is it?" she asks in confusion.

The old lady smiles. "It must be around 3 o'clock, but I'm not sure. I've been here a while too."

"Victoria Díaz?" A woman with short dark hair calls her name again. She's wearing a white coat, and a stethoscope hangs around her neck.

"That's me. I'm Victoria Díaz."

"Come in, please. I'm Dr. Faiman."

The doctor leads her down the hall into a small examination room and motions for her to sit on the table.

"What's wrong?" she asks.

"My throat is burning and so is my forehead. I threw up earlier."

"I'll have a look."

Victoria opens her mouth wide, and the doctor presses her tongue down with a wooden stick, peering at her throat with a small flashlight.

"You have a bad infection. Pull up your top. Let me hear your lungs."

Victoria lifts her top up.

"What are those bruises?"

"Nothing."

"Mmnn . . . did someone hurt you at home?"

"No. I fell down the stairs at school."

"You can trust me and nobody will know."

"I'm okay. Don't worry."

The doctor sighs. "I'll give you something for the infection. It will bring the fever down." She reaches into a cabinet for some pills. "Let's see, today is Friday. Take these pills twice a day for a week, and you'll be okay. Make sure you take them all."

Dr. Faiman walks Victoria to the door. "Now go straight home. You need to rest."

Home? What home, Doctor?

With nowhere to go, Victoria heads toward Centenario School. Halfway there, she stops at Alvear Plaza, feeling dizzy. She finds a water faucet, puts a pill in her mouth and washes it down with tap water. Then she sits down in the sun and spreads the blanket out to dry.

Hunger gnaws at her, but she is too tired to look for food. Her first day without a home. *Pepe won't be at the school tonight. Where will I sleep?*

Victoria thinks of her mother. How every afternoon, after coming home from cleaning rich ladies' houses, she washed clothes in the outdoor sink and sang:

> *Along this path that the heart follows*
> *there is crystal clear water and a burning sun . . .*

The sun is so hot. Victoria wipes sweat from her face.

Mamá would never give up.

Betina once showed Victoria a trophy at a club where she was singing. It was a shining golden woman with open wings and a triumphant pose. "She's called *Winged Victory.*"

Victory. Victoria. That's my name.

Another wave of nausea. Victoria gets up and finds a wooden bench hidden behind trees and shrubs. She lies down on it and covers herself with the blanket.

Help me be victorious, Mamá.

VICTORIA WAKES UP TO THE SINGING OF A *BENTEVEO*. The little bird is perched high at the top of a nearby *Jacarandá* tree preening its yellow and brown feathers. Its song reminds her of being woken by her mother. "Victoria, get up! The *bicho feo* is calling you."

Victoria rubs her eyes and looks around. It's morning, and she has slept all night on the bench.

The benteveo flutters to a puddle, drinks and shakes its funny little head.

"Good morning," Victoria says.

The little bird answers by fluffing out its feathers. Droplets fly through the air.

Victoria goes to the faucet, takes another pill and washes her face. *I feel a bit better today.* She puts the medicine in her pocket, folds the blanket and tucks it under her arm.

She walks down a pathway lined with flowers. Office buildings, a gas station and two museums border the park. The San Miguel church, the Los Andes Café and a few family homes are across the way.

She crosses the plaza to the church and wanders down the streets of a city that doesn't see her. *What can I do?* Desperate for food, she stops at a big white house and rings the bell.

The door opens a crack.

"Can you spare a little something to eat, please?"

The door slams shut, as do the others along the street.

A few metres away, two kids wash the windshield of a car waiting at a stoplight. The driver gives them some coins. The light changes to green, the car leaves and Victoria approaches the kids.

"Hey, che! Can I help wash?"

"No way! It's *our* corner. Don't even think about it."

Everywhere, at each corner, the squeegee kids turn her away.

Famished, Victoria walks back to Alvear Plaza. She stops at Los Andes Café and stares at a half-eaten croissant and an unfinished cup of coffee on one of the outside tables. When the waiter hurries inside, she tucks the croissant inside her shirt.

The waiter comes back and eyes her suspiciously, but he doesn't say anything. He clears a nearby table and takes away the dishes.

Victoria watches him disappear into the café. Inside, next to the cash register, a man with a thick moustache is writing on bits of paper.

Victoria gulps down the leftover coffee. She walks around the corner of the building to eat the croissant.

Suddenly two boys on a motorcycle pull up by the back door. One of them has a gun sticking out of his pocket. They look familiar. *The boys who killed Danny!* The scarred boy climbs off the bike.

Victoria quickly runs to the front of the café and dashes inside. "There's two guys sneaking in the back door and one has a gun," she says to the man behind the register.

"Get in the corner and crouch down," the man says, pulling out a gun. But Victoria is frozen to the spot.

When the boy with the scar walks in, the man behind the counter holds up his gun and barks, "Don't even think about it, or I'll blow your head off!"

Surprised, the boy steps back. He sees Victoria and glares at her, then he turns and runs out the door. Moments later, she sees the motorcycle roar away.

"Thanks, young lady, you saved us," the man says.

Victoria is trembling. *What if they come after me?*

"The exact same thing happened last month," the waiter says. "Those scumbags are everywhere."

"And if they're on drugs, even worse," the man says.

"You owe her a big one, Moustache," says a guy coming out of the storeroom.

"You're right, Cacho," he says, putting his gun away. "Make her a latte and bring some croissants. Have a seat."

"What's your name?" the waiter asks, bringing her the food.

"Victoria."

"I'm Beto and Cacho's the cook."

Moustache sits down beside her. "Where do you live?"

"On the street."

"And your parents?"

"My mom was killed," Victoria begins and finds it hard to go on.

"And your father?" Beto gently sets a latte down on the table.

"He . . . he left and never showed up again."

"Poor girl. Don't you have any other family?"

"I don't have anyone."

"You know what?" Moustache says. "We could use someone to clean up at night after we close. Do you want a job? You can sleep in the storeroom. We'll feed you breakfast. But you can't hang around here during the day. What do you say?"

"I'll do it. Thanks!"

"Beto, take her back and show her the storeroom. Cacho, bring her a sandwich for later." He holds out his hand for Victoria. "Shake."

CHAPTER FOUR

A LITTLE LATER, VICTORIA SITS ON A BENCH IN THE PLAZA. She nibbles at the sandwich, hoping to keep it down.

A tall skinny boy about her age takes a seat next to her. "What's your name?" he asks.

She takes a bite out of the sandwich without answering.

"Tasty?"

Victoria nods and avoids his eyes.

"I'm Marko."

Chewing slowly, she glances his way. He's wearing a black and yellow striped cap on top of a head of curly hair.

"I haven't seen you before."

Victoria swallows. "I just came."

"Marko with a *k*. And not Marco*s*. It ends in an *o*: *M-a-r-K-o*."

"I'm Victoria. Victoria with a *c*, ending in an *a*."

He laughs. "You're funny."

"No. I'm Victoria. Are you stupid?"

"No. I'm Marko."

They laugh.

"Do you live around here?"

"I sleep at that café." She nods in the direction of Los Andes.

"I've been watching you. A pretty *chiquilina* like you doesn't show up on the streets every day."

"Got nothing else to do but watch?"

"I wash car windows with that *botija* at the corner." He points.

"I asked so many squeegee kids if I could work with them, and they all said no."

"You can work with me. I'll fix it up with the Captain."

"Who's the Captain?"

"He's the boss, *vo*. He owns all the corners around here."

"You talk funny. Where are you from?"

"Montevideo."

"How did you end up here?"

"It's a long story."

Marko takes off his cap and runs his fingers through his curls. Then he puts it on again, backwards.

"What's that black and yellow label on your hat?"

"I support Peñarol. I'm a coal man till death do us part, vo." He kicks a pebble towards an imaginary soccer goal.

"Why a coal man?"

"Because the first players worked shovelling coal onto the trains. Something like that."

"Oh, but now that you live here you should root for an Argentine team, che."

"I know. I like the River team. I watched some of their games."

"Nooooooooo! Not the River team! Their mascot is a chicken! You have to be a *bostero*, like me."

"I see. So I have to support Boca if I'm going to be your friend?"

"Yeah."

Marko gives her a nudge. "Just look at me talking about soccer with a girl."

"You mean girls know nothing about soccer?"

"So what do you say? D'you wanna wash cars with me or not?"

"You bet."

Marko goes over to a boy washing the windshield of a black Honda station wagon and says to him, "Hey, Chichón, Cogote is looking for someone to help at Five Corners. Beat it!"

The boy takes off at a run, and Marko waves Victoria over. He soaks a rag in a bucket of dirty water and wrings it out. "When the cars stop, start washing their windows. Here, grab a rag."

Victoria nods, sticks her hand into the grey scummy water, and pulls out a scrap of cloth.

Marko points to a car. "That one's yours."

Victoria rushes over to it and throws the rag onto the car's windshield.

"No! No! No! It's already been washed!" the driver shouts, sticking his head out the window.

The stop light changes and the cars move. Marko shouts insults at the man as he drives away. Then he throws his rag into the bucket and comes up to Victoria. "As my granny used to say, a nice car can't hide the idiot inside."

Victoria laughs.

When the light turns red again, she sings while she scrubs the window of a brand-new Fiat.

> *There you go alone in your car,*
> *acting like a king,*
> *making all sorts of plans*
> *for the girls that you see on the way . . .*

"I like your singing," the man says smiling, and he hands her a couple of coins.

Marko looks over. "You're doing a great job."

In the afternoon, Victoria feels a wave of dizziness and worries she will throw up. But the spell passes. Car after car, hour after hour, her hands move to the rhythm of the tangos that her mother taught her. As she washes a Volkswagen Beetle, she sings:

Who was that quirky bug
who said to you, che, man,
it's past the time to dance?

Marko laughs. "You're completely crazy, chiquilina!" He trots to a rusty Peugeot 505, leaving a Renault Clio to Victoria. When she's done, she runs up to the next car, but the driver says, "Leave it, girl. I want to talk with the Uruguayan."

She whistles to Marko. He hurries over, pulls a small bag from his pocket and hands it to the driver. The man gives Marko a bill, revs his engine three times and, without waiting for the green light, peels off at top speed.

"Dinner's on me, chiquilina," Marko says. "It's part of your welcome package. Here." He hands her the water bucket. "Take this over to the café and leave it there, so I don't have to keep it with me overnight. I'll wait for you here, *ta?*"

When she returns, he pulls a joint out of his pocket, lights it and offers it to her.

"No. Are you crazy? Why do you smoke that crap?"

Marko shrugs and starts walking down the street. "Why does it bug you so much?"

"My father took drugs, that sick bastard," Victoria says. The hatred she has been holding onto for so long comes flooding out. "He killed my mother. One day he came home really wasted and beat her so she would say where she hid her money. She wouldn't tell him. It was all we had. He kept hitting her until she collapsed. My cousin, Betina, and I took her to the hospital, and the doctor said she was in a coma. She never woke up."

"That's really terrible, vo. Where's your father now?"

"He took off because he didn't want to go to jail, and because he doesn't dare look me in the eye. He sent my aunt a letter saying that he was in Brazil. I don't care where he is. I never want to see him again."

"Have you got any brothers or sisters?"

"I've got two brothers—they're twins. They're going to be six."

"Here we are," Marko says, leading her around the side of the Bambino Pizza Parlour. He snuffs out the joint against the wall and walks inside. Victoria follows. The place smells of cheese, olive oil, tomato sauce, herbs and spices.

A young man with a white hat moves past them with a huge bag of flour on his shoulder. Without taking his eyes off of Victoria, he says, "Hey, Botija, how's it going?"

"Whatcha doing, Tuco?" Marko says. "Do you have anything for me, vo? Where's Bambino?"

"Dunno." Tuco sets down the flour. "Pop in another Mozzarella," he says to a couple of guys loading a brick oven with pizzas. "Who's the pretty girl?"

"Her name's Victoria. And she's with me."

"Hey, dude, take it easy."

"I'm going to the washroom," Marko says. "Don't get too friendly with her while I'm gone."

Tuco wipes his hands on his apron and gives Victoria a greeting kiss.

When Marko comes back, one of the pizza boys hands him a paperboard box, and Tuco gives him a beer from the fridge.

"Thanks, vo. Tell Bambino I was here."

Victoria and Marko sit with their backs against the wall of Nacional High School. Marko opens the box, and Victoria takes a slice.

"Why did that guy call you Botija?"

"Because I say it a lot. In Uruguay we call all the young kids botija."

Marko opens the bottle of beer with his teeth, takes a drink and hands it to Victoria. She hesitates, then decides to try it. It's bitter but quenches her thirst.

"So you were telling me about your little brothers. Where are they?"

"They're with my aunt."

"Don't you live there too?"

"Not anymore."

"How come?"

Victoria shrugs her shoulders. "My aunt's boyfriend bothered me. Lots of times."

"Like how?"

"He grabbed me. He wanted to do . . . whatever."

"I can see why you ran away. What do you do over at the café?"

"I'm gonna clean the floors and the bathroom. Where do you live?"

"In a shed with other botijas. One day I'm going to open my own flower shop in Montevideo."

"One day I'm going to go back to school. It's my dream to be a teacher."

"We all have dreams. My grandma always wanted me to be a doctor, but having a flower shop is enough for me. My mother can help me. She's crazy about flowers."

"That's a good idea. What are you waiting for, *boludo*?"

"For you to come with me," he says, smiling.

Victoria laughs and takes another piece of pizza. Marko takes the last sip of beer.

"So why did you come to Paraná?"

"Because I was stupid. One of my father's old friends asked me if I wanted to come here and make some money. He said I'd make my mom proud. He said they had a job for me in their flower shop. I worked there for two months, then their son came back from Buenos Aires, so they got rid of me. I'll go back home as soon as I save up enough."

Marko takes off his cap and puts the day's take into it. "We'll work as a team. Put your dough in the hat."

Victoria puts her money in too. Marko counts the pile of cash and divides it into three. "Half goes to the Captain. We split the rest."

"Half goes to the Captain?"

"I told you, he's the boss. He gets his part of the take. Meet you at the corner tomorrow morning, ta?" He offers his fist to Victoria, and she touches it with hers. Then he walks away, turns around and blows her a kiss.

I like that Marko.

VICTORIA SITS ON A BENCH ACROSS FROM THE CAFÉ AT Alvear Plaza and counts her money. When Beto begins setting chairs upside down on the outside tables, she joins him in the clean-up.

Saturday. My second day without my brothers, without a home.

She takes her medicine and finishes putting dishes away.

Aunt Marta's wasn't a home.

Beto shouts a good-bye. The café is quiet and dark. Victoria sets a piece of cardboard on the floor of the storeroom between boxes and shelves and lies down, covering herself with Pepperoni's blanket.

CHAPTER FIVE

VICTORIA WAKES UP, STARTLED. SHE HAD BEEN DREAMING about a fight between gangs in front of her aunt's house. It is only Beto, carrying a box of bottles into the storeroom.

"Time to get up, sleepyhead, we're about to open," the waiter says. He has a guitar on his back, and he tries not to bump it against anything as he sets the bottles on a shelf.

"Okay, okay," Victoria says, stretching. "What's with the guitar?"

"I have a party after work. Now hurry up, che. It's a nice day."

"Breakfast is ready, Victoria!" Cacho shouts from the kitchen.

She can't help smiling at how loud he is. *These guys are so kind!* She quickly gulps a pill, washes up and follows Beto into the café.

As Victoria fills the bucket at the plaza's faucet, she looks around for Marko. He's nowhere to be seen. *It's no use waiting.* She walks over to the corner and starts washing car windows.

A woman with short grey hair, wearing a dark dress buttoned up the front and black sensible shoes, walks out of San Miguel Church. Victoria recognizes her. "Doña Frida!" she shouts, dropping her rag and running across the street.

The woman looks up, surprised. "Do I know you?"

"I'm Susy's daughter. You remember me, don't you? My mother used to clean for you."

"Victoria! Is that you, darling?" Doña Frida kisses her on the cheek. "How are those handsome young brothers of yours?"

"They're big now. They'll be six this year."

"I heard about your poor mother. I'm so sorry." She hugs Victoria. "Are you well? Where are you living?"

"With my aunt," Victoria lies.

Doña Frida takes a bill folded into four from her bra and gently closes Victoria's hand on the money. "Please keep it and come visit me whenever you want. You know where I live. Bring the twins."

"I will. Thank you." Victoria kisses Doña Frida goodbye and walks away slowly, so she won't be seen heading to the corner to wash cars.

At midday Marko shows up and starts washing as if he had been at it all morning.

"Where have you been?"

"Church."

"Church?"

"Of course not." He laughs. "I had some business with the Captain, vo. I got everything fixed up for you, chiquilina."

The driver of a beat-up truck calls Marko to him. They hit fists and chat a bit.

It seems to Victoria like they're speaking in code. She tries to hear what they are saying, but they're talking too quietly. She turns away and cleans the windshield of a flaming red Mercedes. The woman hands her some coins. Her arm is decorated with colourful jewellery. "You shouldn't be washing car windows. Don't you go to school?"

Victoria opens her mouth to answer, but the woman speeds off.

I used to go to school. And I used to do special things with Mamá and the twins on Sundays. We'd visit Great Aunt Raquel or go for an ice cream.

Around two o'clock, Marko comes up to her. "It's time for a break."

Victoria looks at him with relief. "Let me treat you to a meal. I have enough for a couple of hot dogs and pop," she says.

"Save it, vo. I know a place where we can get something to eat." Marko takes the bucket to the magazine kiosk around the corner. The boy behind the counter opens the side door and steps out to greet Marko. He's tall with a broad back and shoulders, his hair slicked up with gel. He's wearing the Argentine national soccer team jersey.

Marko hands him the bucket and says, "Hey Andrés, keep this for me. Back in an hour."

The boy looks at Victoria and smiles. "New helper?"

"Yeah. She's Victoria."

"*Victoria Alada*! Winged Victory! Just like my trophy.'"

"Your trophy?" Victoria asks.

"Yeah, che. For my skill at soccer."

Andrés tries to give Victoria a greeting kiss, but Marko steps in between them. "We're hungry man, gotta go. Back soon." He grabs Victoria by the elbow, turns and leads her down the street.

Urquiza Park is full of people enjoying the sun. Children play with a ball, couples stroll hand-in-hand, teenagers bike past blasting music. Marko and Victoria pass by the statue of the Indian girl holding an arrow.

So different from the night I ran away.

"Are you daydreaming, vo?" Marko asks.

Victoria shakes her head. She and Marko run down a pathway through the ravine to a hotdog stand on the esplanade by the river. "I want a couple of hotdogs and two pops. Take it off the money you owe the Captain," Marko says to the vendor, opening a cooler and helping himself to two cans.

"Let's go somewhere quiet to eat," Victoria says.

They make their way along the esplanade and find a spot to sit on the low wall separating the river from the city. Swinging their legs, they look out over the water. A small group of teenage girls saunter by on the walkway behind them, drinking mate and talking about their teachers.

"Did you ever go to school?" Victoria asks, taking a bite out of her hotdog.

"Only sometimes. I had to work to support my mom. My grandma needed a whole pile of medicine, and there were three of us to feed." Marko takes off his cap and wipes his forehead with the back of his hand.

A black dog with dark shining eyes trots up to Victoria and she pets him.

"You know, one day the teacher came to my house," Marko continues. "He made a big speech about how, by law, kids have to go to school. So I asked him if 'the law' would give me money to support my family."

"And what did he say?"

"That if I went to school it would help me get a better job to make more money."

"Well, that's true, che."

"Yeah, like I said, my grandma wanted me to be a doctor." He hangs his head and mutters, "But what do I know? And my mother never earned enough to even feed us."

"What about your father?"

"No idea. The only thing I know is that when I was two, he ran off with another woman and never came back."

"Did you ever look for him?"

"Why bother? He knows where we live."

"Maybe you're better off without him."

Marko shrugs.

Victoria picks up a stick from the ground and throws it for the black dog to chase after. The dog barks and fetches it.

"So you like dogs?"

"Yeah, a lot," Victoria says, breaking off a bit of her hotdog and tossing it to the dog.

After eating, she and Marko watch the *camalotes* floating down the river. Marko takes out a small photograph from his back pocket and looks at it for a few seconds. He hands it to her. It's a picture of him as a little boy being held by a woman. There's a tiny black and white pup by the woman's side.

"That's a really nice picture," Victoria says, handing it back. "Is that your mother?"

"Yes. And that's Momo," Marko says, pointing to the dog. He jumps off the wall and slips his arm around Victoria. Surprised, she isn't sure how to respond. "We could catch a movie tonight," he suggests.

"Are you crazy? Movies are way too expensive."

Marko laughs. "There's a store on the *peatonal* that sells TVs. We can watch it through the window."

AFTER SIESTA, THEY WORK WITHOUT STOPPING FOR THE REST of the afternoon. When twilight comes, Marko wrings out the rags, dumps the dirty water into the gutter and says, "That's it for the day."

Victoria drops the bucket off at the café, and Beto hollers, "Hey, girl!" He hands her a brown paper bag. "This is for you."

She opens the bag. It's filled with leftover white bread sandwiches. "Thanks, che!"

The once bustling shops now have their shutters closed tight. Marko and Victoria join a group of people standing in front of the big window of an appliance store. Its shutter was open, allowing everyone to see the televisions inside.

"That's a good show, Botija! The one with a magician."

They sit down on the edge of a flowerbed facing the shop. Placing the bag of food between them, Marko says, "You want to see some real magic? Watch me make my sandwich disappear."

Victoria laughs. She loves the show on television.

Marko says something, but Victoria's not listening. She's spellbound by the magician's tricks. A clown interrupts the show, pretending to be a magician, and she laughs and laughs.

A group of teenagers walk past singing, a couple kiss on a bench in the gazebo in the middle of the peatonal, a policeman twirls his nightstick as he strides by, and an old man pushes a cart overflowing with cardboard boxes. *It isn't Pepperoni.*

The streets thin out. Marko falls asleep.

Victoria tries to wake him. "Hey, che! I've got to get back to the café before they close, or I won't be able to get in." She gives him a nudge, but he doesn't wake up. Finally she runs off, leaving him fast asleep.

ONLY CACHO IS STILL AT LOS ANDES. VICTORIA GOES OVER to him. He's filling out a shopping list for the next day. He looks up and smiles at her. "At last! I thought you weren't coming. I was just about to lock up."

"Yeah, I was watching TV on the peatonal and . . . "

"Make sure you watch the time. You don't want to sleep on the street again. I'm going home now. *Chau*, che."

"Chau, man. I'll clean up, then I'm going to bed."

"Okay. Leave everything spotless."

She nods. "You better come with sunglasses tomorrow, so the shiny floor doesn't hurt your eyes."

Cacho laughs and leaves, locking up the café.

As Victoria sweeps up the crumbs, peanut shells, paper napkins and pop tops, she thinks about the twins, and feels overwhelmed with guilt for leaving them. "I'm so sorry," she says, leaning on the broom, and cries.

CHAPTER SIX

"Good morning," says Moustache, coming into the storeroom with a thin mattress. "Here's a present for you, che."

"Thank you, boss!" Victoria jumps up and kisses his cheek.

"Okay, okay, but don't ask me for anything when you get married," Moustache says, laughing. He rolls up the mattress and leaves it between two piles of wooden boxes and goes into the kitchen.

At the traffic light, businessmen straighten their ties, young people sing, ladies fuss with their hair and dogs of all sizes and shapes pant in the heat.

Whenever a car pulls up, Victoria entertains herself by trying to guess who she'll find on the other side of the glass.

Most drivers hand her a few coins. Once in a while, they smile or nod as well.

During a break in traffic, she sits down on the curb next to the bucket to rest. *Another morning without Marko. And he'll still want his share of the take.*

Victoria recognizes a familiar face across the street. Her stomach twists and flips. *It's the guy with the scar—the one who killed Danny.*

The boy stands and stares at her. She doesn't know what to do, but then the boy who used to work the corner walks by.

"Hey, Chichón!" she yells. She glances back, looking for the boy with the scar. But he's gone.

"How do you know my name?"

"I heard Marko call you that."

"Oh, yeah. Everything okay? You look nervous."

"Yeah, sure. I'm sorry Marko made you go to Five Corners because of me."

"Nah, it's all good. I'm okay with Cogote, and we do alright over there." He sits down next to her. "They call me Chichón because I'm short. What's your name?

"They call me Victoria because . . . I'm victorious."

"That's a good one, che. Where's Marko?"

Victoria hugs her legs and leans her chin on her knees. "He's late again. I'm here all alone. Do you want to work here with me?"

"Sure."

The light turns yellow, and they run out to the cars with their rags.

It's well after noon, and Chichón's tummy is making noisy rumbling sounds.

"Your alarm clock is telling us it's time to eat," Victoria says. "Let's take a break."

She gestures for Chichón to follow her, and they walk to the café and knock on the back door. Beto steps outside, and with a welcoming smile, he hands Victoria a couple of leftover sandwiches.

"Thanks, che."

"Hey, Vicky! You got a new boyfriend?"

"Chichón's just a friend." She laughs. "And don't call me Vicky. I don't really like it."

On their way back to the corner, Victoria sees her aunt's neighbour walking past.

Victoria hesitates. "Wait here," she says to Chichón. Then she runs over to the woman. "Hi, Lily."

"Oh, it's you, is it?" Lily says, looking astonished. "Marta told me you ran away."

"Yes. But please, don't tell her you saw me."

"Why would I? Marta's already told me all about how ungrateful you are. It's lucky your brothers have my kids to play with, or I don't know what she'd do, working so hard."

"Are my brothers okay?"

"Of course they are," Lily snaps.

"Please tell the twins I'm okay, and that I love them." Victoria's voice breaks.

But Lily doesn't hear. She's walking away.

Chichón and Victoria sit down at a bench in the plaza to have their lunch.

"Who was that woman?" Chichón asks.

"No one," Victoria says. "An old neighbour. Where do you sleep, che?"

"Over by Bajada Grande at a warehouse."

"Do you live with your parents there?"

"My uncle's my only family." Chichón stuffs the last piece of the sandwich into his mouth and mumbles, "I'd better get over to Five Corners otherwise Cogote's gonna be mad at me."

Victoria works alone for the rest of the afternoon. As the sun slips behind the rooftops, a fluorescent green motorcycle pulls up, tires squealing. The driver wears black sunglasses. His passenger jumps off. He's a creepy mean-looking guy with a mouth full of black teeth. "Where's Marko?" he bellows.

"I don't know," Victoria says, startled.

"The Captain wants his money. If Marko doesn't bring it to him today, he's a dead man. You tell him that." The guy jumps back on the bike, and it disappears into the flow of traffic.

Victoria grabs the bucket and rushes to the kiosk. "Have you seen Marko?" she asks the boy at the stand.

"No, che," he says. He's wearing a different soccer jersey today.

"Do you know where he is? He didn't show up. I'm worried."

"Get used to it. He comes and goes. He's involved in all kinds of things, and they're not all on the up and up."

"The up and up?"

"Legal, if you know what I mean." He takes the bucket. "I'll put that away. My name's Andrés."

"I remember, and I remember you play soccer too."

"You're right. I'm going professional."

"Professional?"

"I've had a couple of tryouts with the big teams. And I'm heading for one with Patronato right now."

"Really? Do you have a chance?"

"It's the third time I've been called back. Who knows?" He shrugs, stepping out of the newspaper stand and locking it. "I gotta go. I need to be on time." He unlocks a red motorcycle parked next to the stand.

"Nice bike. Yours?"

Andrés laughs. "No. It's Gringo's."

"Gringo?"

"He owns the stand. He lets me use his bike to deliver newspapers every morning. He's supposed to be here by now to take over."

"I saw Gringo crossing the plaza, walking this way," says Marko, coming up from the corner. "Don't mess with my girl, you little Maradona."

"Who says I'm your girl, che?" Victoria interrupts. "Where have you been?"

"I gotta go," Andrés says. He starts the motorcycle, jumps on and takes off. At the corner he waves at Gringo, who walks up to the stand, unlocks the side door and goes in.

"So where have you been, Botija?" Victoria asks again.

"Business."

"A guy came by looking for you. He said the Captain wants his money right away. I hope you know what you're doing."

"I do, and I don't need you or anyone to tell me what to do. I saw the Captain already. It's all sorted out." Marko takes her arm. "Let's get something to eat. I know the guy at the bar across from the post office."

"Does he owe you money too?"

"He's my friend. Let's go."

WHEN THEY GET TO THE BAR, MARKO KNOCKS ON A WINDOW darkened by grease. A young man with long straggly hair opens it. "Wait there, Botija," he says.

A few minutes later, he opens the window and hands Marko a cardboard box and two cans of pop.

"Let's go to the Cathedral," Marko says. They walk in silence. They sit down on the Cathedral steps and start to eat. When Marko puts an arm around her, Victoria gets up and shakes the crumbs off her clothes. Pigeons jump at them, squawking and squabbling.

Then she sees him again. *The boy with the scar.* She grabs Marko's arm.

"What's wrong, chiquilina?"

"That boy over there," she says. "He's been following me."

"Following you, why?"

"I saw him and another guy kill Danny, my neighbour. They turned up at the café the other day, looking for trouble."

"Oh, Mate Cosido! He's bad news," Marko says. "I'll get rid of that hijo de puta—you wait here."

He walks down the steps to the boy. They talk heatedly, and the boy stalks off.

"He won't be bothering you anymore. Don't worry."

"What did you say to him?"

Marko shrugs and takes her arm. "He owes me some favours. Let's go."

They go to the shop with the TVs in the window and elbow their way to the front. It's a car chase. A James Bond type of action hero is racing through dunes and past palm trees.

When the movie is over, Marko puts his arm around Victoria again. This time he pulls her close. She shrugs him off. The disappointment shows in his face. "Are you mad at me?"

"No. I'm just worried."

"About what?"

"Everything. I worry about my brothers, the twins. I worry about that guy. I worry about you."

Marko laughs. "You worry about me? That's good, because I like you."

They stop by the fountain in the middle of Alvear Plaza. Large stone mermaids hold cone-shaped seashells to their lips. Marko says, "It looks like they are slurping ice cream from the bottom of the cone."

He slips his hand in the water and splashes Victoria; she laughs and pretends to run away. He chases her and tries to kiss her, but she breaks away and says, "I don't want to be late. Last night I was almost locked out."

When they reach the café, Marko asks, "Where's the money from today?"

"Here," she says, handing it to him.

"I'd better go."

"What about my share?" Victoria demands.

"I'll fix it up with you. I need it till tomorrow." He puts the money away and walks down the street with his hands in his pockets.

CHAPTER SEVEN

EVERY DAY OVER THE NEXT TWO WEEKS, MARKO ARRIVES late at the corner. And every day, after they finish work, Marko borrows Victoria's share of the money they earn.

Finally, tired and frustrated, Victoria confronts him. "Do you have my money? I want it now!"

"You got up on the wrong side of the bed," Marko says.

"If I had a bed."

He takes out a plastic bag of white powder. "How about some of this?" he says, offering her some.

"You know I don't do drugs."

"How about a kiss then?" He grabs her.

She pushes him away. "You're totally wasted. Get off me."

"Don't get all worked up. I'm just messing around." Marko laughs.

"What are you doing with that stuff?"

"I have to drop it off."

Victoria shakes her head. "You'd better get my money soon."

A white taxi and a dirty Ford station wagon pull up. Marko grabs his rag and heads for the Ford, and Victoria takes her rag over to the taxi.

AT NOON CHICHÓN COMES BY AND SITS ON THE CURB.

"You're just in time. I've got an errand to do. Stick around and help Victoria here," Marko says, tossing him his rag.

Chichón catches it. "Whatever you say."

"Thanks, che!" Marko shouts, weaving between the cars.

"Watch yourself!" Victoria calls. But he's already gone.

Chichón goes up to an old dented Renault. But the moment he leans over the windshield, he throws up and staggers away.

"You idiot!" the driver yells.

Victoria rushes to the car, cleans up the mess and goes to Chichón. "Sick?"

He's trembling and bathed in sweat. "I don't know. A little while ago I started to feel like crap."

"What did you take?"

"Just glue."

"Glue! You wanna die? Lie down there against the wall."

"No. The Captain will get mad if I don't make any money."

"So let him get mad. Rest for a bit. You can go back to work later."

She throws the dirty water in the gutter and takes the bucket to the kiosk. Gringo, the owner, is there.

"Where's Andrés?" Victoria asks.

"He's off today."

"Do you have a towel I could use? My friend is sick."

"Sure." He hands her a washcloth.

She thanks him and hurries back to the plaza. Picking up an empty plastic bottle from the garbage can, she goes to the water faucet, soaks the towel, fills up the bottle and returns to Chichón. She kneels beside him and offers him a drink. As he takes a sip, she says, "Here, clean yourself a little, and I'll take you home."

"No, you keep working, or the Captain will get mad. I'll lie down for a bit here and see if it goes away."

"Let's quit for the day. We can go over to the plaza, find some shade and rest. If you don't feel better, I'll take you to your uncle's place."

AT THE PLAZA, THEY DROP DOWN ONTO A BENCH AND REST their heads against its wooden arms. Victoria's thoughts fly up to the treetops. A breeze rocks the branches, and soon she and Chichón fall asleep.

Victoria is woken by someone grabbing at her. "Get off

me," she yells in panic and is greeted by laughter.

A group of young people are standing over her, drinking beer. One of them slips and falls on top of Victoria. He laughs and laughs as she tries to push him off.

"Leave us alone!" Chichón shouts, standing up.

"Hey *piojito*," mocks the youngest-looking member of the group, "if you want to be alone with your girlfriend, you should go somewhere else." He glances at the others for approval.

"Let's go, you're gonna make the piojito cry," a tall guy says, pulling his friend off Victoria.

"Yeah, we shouldn't waste bullets on little birds."

They stumble off, staggering and turning around every so often to yell and laugh.

Victoria gets up and shakes herself. "They're such jerks," she says, watching them as they throw beer bottles into the fountain. "Being a boy, things must be easier for you on the street."

Chichón takes a deep breath. "I'm not a boy."

"What do you mean you're not a boy? Are you kidding me, boludo?"

Chichón blushes. "I'm serious, believe me. It's the truth."

"But why are you dressed like a boy?" Victoria looks hard at Chichón, trying to see her as a girl.

"Like you said, it's easier being a boy on the street."

"Wow! Does Marko know?"

"No one knows. Only my uncle. He started dressing me like this and treating me like a boy a long time ago."

Victoria can't stop staring. "I'm speechless, che."

Chichón shrugs.

Victoria still can't believe it. *How strange!*

"That's not the worst thing he does to me." Tears well up in Chichón's eyes.

Horrible. Just like Juan. "Why don't you run away?"

"I've tried. Every time I go, he finds me and beats me like crazy. But I have a plan."

"What is it?"

"Next time I run, I'm getting out of town. I'm going to Rosario."

"Rosario?"

"I met a lady who wants to help me. She says I can work in her bakery. She drives back and forth from Rosario every month to help her sick mom. She's promised to take me with her next time she comes."

"Wow! Sounds perfect."

"Please don't tell Marko or anyone else that I'm a girl. I told you because I've been wanting to tell someone for a long time, and you're the first girl who's been working with us. And besides, you're so nice."

"I swear I won't say a word," Victoria promises, kissing her index finger and making the sign of the cross over her lips.

Late in the afternoon, Marko turns up, hands in his pockets, kicking a crushed soda can.

"I guess it was *really* far away where you had to go to drop off that package," Victoria says, swatting him with her rag.

"I had other things to do. By the way, here's your money," he says, handing it to her. He empties the dirty water from the bucket onto the street. "Let's get out of here. I'm hungry."

"You have to take me to a real fancy restaurant today to make up for not showing up. Not to one of your so-called friends who owe you something."

"Okay, okay. Let's go to a fancy place." He laughs, and stops abruptly, looking over her shoulder. "It's the Captain. You wait here. I'll be right back."

The Captain is tall and beefy, dressed in army clothes. He has a bulky gold chain hanging around his neck and rings on every finger. *He looks mean, like Juan.*

The Captain grabs Marko and starts shouting. Marko hurriedly reaches into his pocket and hands him something. Then he saunters back to Victoria, looking sheepish.

"I thought you saw him yesterday."

"I did, but I didn't have everything I owed him."

"So you have no money left."

"Sorry. We'll have to get a pizza from Tuco."

THEY GO TO SIRIRÍ DUCK PARK WITH THE PIZZA AND SIT sideways on two swings, so they face each other. As they eat, Victoria daydreams about the times she came to the park with her mother and the twins.

Marko nudges her with his foot. "So how come you don't like me?"

"I do, but I don't want to be more than friends with you."

"You *do* like me. I knew it."

"You're a lot of trouble, you know that, Botija?" she says, smiling and giving him a soft punch on the shoulder.

THE CAFÉ IS DARK, AND IT SEEMS LIKE NO ONE IS THERE. Victoria tries both doors. "Ay! It's locked. What am I going to do?"

"I'll take care of you. Come with me."

"Where?"

"I know a place where we can sleep. It's safe and it has way more than five stars," he says, laughing. "Tomorrow you can come here early and do your cleanup before they open for business."

MARKO TAKES HER HAND. HE LEADS HER UP AND DOWN THE cement staircases that cut like scars through the ravines of

Urquiza Park to a clearing behind some bushes and palms. He lies down on a bench and gestures to her. Victoria joins him and rests her head on his shoulder. She listens for footsteps, for taunting voices.

Another day away from the twins. Guilt sweeps over her.

It takes her a long time to fall asleep.

CHAPTER EIGHT

Victoria gets to the café just as Cacho is opening up. "Hey, where were you last night?" he asks.

"Sorry, I came too late. I'll clean up now."

"Out with your boyfriend, huh?" He hands her a broom. She sweeps up.

Beto brings a latte and a croissant for each of them. "That guy you're with is no good," Beto says. "He deals drugs."

"He helped me get the job."

"So what? Guys like that end up dead."

At the corner, Victoria finds Marko playing with Bite'm.

"This little puppy wandered over here. I never gave you a present, so do you want him?" Marko asks.

"That's Bite'm." She lifts up the puppy, kisses it and asks, "Where's Pepperoni and Brownie?"

The puppy licks her cheek and wags its tail.

"I'm really happy to see you too. What are you doing on your own?"

"He looks like my dog Momo. We could call him Momo."

"No, his name's Bite'm, *estúpido!*"

"We could call him Pirate because of the patch on his eye. Or Asphalt Pirate 'cause he's a street dog," Andrés says, coming up behind them.

"No. We'll call him Bite'm. That's his name," Victoria insists.

As Andrés bends down to play with the puppy, the green motorcycle pulls up. The Captain is driving.

"Marko! Get on," the Captain orders. "We've got business."

Marko jumps on, and the bike speeds off. Andrés and Victoria walk to the magazine stand.

"He's getting in deeper and deeper with the Captain," Andrés says. He picks up a stack of newspapers and disappears with them inside the kiosk. "You don't need to be with a guy like that," he adds, looking out from the front of the stand. He flashes her a wide smile.

Suddenly high-pitched howls and furious barking erupt from the corner. Four big street dogs, with scabby skin and bald splotches, surround Bite'm.

Victoria grabs a rock, rushes over and throws it at the pack. "*Fuera*!" she shouts. When she bends down to scoop up the puppy, her foot catches on the uneven sidewalk, and she sprawls onto the street. Cars skid to a stop, brakes screeching. A bus swerves. Victoria holds the little dog tight. "We're okay, boy. We're okay."

Bite'm licks her hand.

She feels a strong grip pull her to safety. "Are you alright?" Andrés asks, brushing the dust from her hair. "Come with me."

At the stand, he gives her a bottle of water and puts out a bowl for the puppy. "You're always getting into trouble, *muñeca*, aren't you? You need someone to watch over you day and night."

Victoria laughs. "Are you volunteering for the job?"

He gives her a serious look. "Maybe."

After work, Victoria drops the bucket off at the café and heads to Centenario School to see if she can find Pepperoni and return the puppy. There is no sign of the old man at the school. Bite'm bounds up the steps, sniffs around and lies down in the spot where his owner slept the night Victoria met him.

"Bite'm!" the custodian exclaims, coming out to lock the school door.

"Mister, have you seen Pepperoni, the guy who sleeps here, the one with the cart?"

The custodian puts his hand over his eyes and rubs his forehead. "I have bad news. He was hit by a car last night."

Victoria's heart sinks. "Is he in the hospital?" she asks. "I want to give Bite'm back to him."

"I'm afraid he died in the accident. Brownie too," the man says, touching her shoulder.

"WHY ARE YOU CRYING?" IT'S ANDRÉS. HE'S ARRIVED AT THE Plaza carrying a basket of flowers. He sits down beside Victoria on the bench and puts an arm around her.

Stifling a sob, she leans into his shoulder and says, "Bite'm's owner was killed last night." She pets the little puppy curled up on her lap.

"How terrible. Who was he?"

"An old man who lived on the streets. He was kind to me."

"I'm so sorry." He takes a sprig of jasmine from his basket and gently places it behind her ear.

"What's this for?"

"To cheer up a pretty girl."

He's sweet. Despite her sadness, Victoria can see that Andrés is brimming with something to say. "You look like you have better news than me."

"I do. I'm gonna play for Patronato." A huge grin spreads across Andrés' face.

"You made it! That's awesome, che. When are you gonna start?"

"Don't know yet. I made the team is all I know."

"That's wonderful. I'm so happy for you." She looks at his basket of flowers. "Where are you going with those?"

"I get them from an Italian man, and I sell them in the bars at night."

"That sounds like fun."

"Do you want to help me?"

She pauses, thinking his offer over. "Sure, why not?"

"Great. Let's get more flowers for you to sell."

As they walk, Victoria tells Andrés about Pepperoni and how he helped her the night she ran away from her aunt's house.

"Sounds like he was a nice man," Andrés says.

"He was like a magician. He could pull all sorts of things out of his cart," Victoria says.

On Perú Street, Andrés points to a small flower shop saying, "That's the place where Marko used to work."

Victoria shakes her head. "Hijos de puta. It's their fault Botija ended up with the Captain."

In front of the cemetery, they stop at a whitewashed house with a tin roof and two barred windows on either side of a red door. Andrés pounds at it and waits.

A few seconds later, the door opens and a bald chubby man emerges wearing a wrinkled white shirt, pyjama bottoms and slippers. "Hey, *amico*! *Come vai*? Who's the *ragazza* with the little dog?"

"She's Victoria and the puppy is Bite'm."

"Don't call him that in front of clients, you'll scare them," the man says, laughing.

"Look, Tano," says Andrés, "I'm going to teach her to sell flowers. Is that okay with you?"

"Hey, why would I have a problem with that? The more kids selling, the better. Right, *bellezza*? Here's some for you." He hands Victoria a basket.

Bite'm wags his tail.

On their way downtown, Andrés gives Victoria a few tips. "Go for the couples. Guys always have money to spend on their dates. Try saying things like, 'Every *princesa* deserves a beautiful flower.' You'll get the idea."

At first Victoria just watches Andrés, but then she goes out with Bite'm on her own. She enjoys selling flowers. She likes their scent and the girls' smiles when they're given posies. And most of all, she likes being close to Andrés. *This is much better than washing windshields.*

THERE ARE STILL CUSTOMERS IN THE CAFÉ WHEN VICTORIA returns. She picks up some leftover food from a table

Beto hasn't cleared to give to Bite'm. He gobbles it up gratefully.

You're so little—like my brothers. I need to see them soon.

Victoria wanders outside to Alvear Plaza. When she sits down on a bench, Bite'm jumps eagerly onto her lap and falls asleep. She strokes his head.

I don't know what I would have done without you that night, little puppy—you and Brownie and Pepperoni.

Looking up at the sky, she sings:

> *Come—you said to me sadly—*
> *my soul can bear no more*
> *of this loneliness.*
> *Come, and take pity on my pain.*
> *I am tired of crying*
> *of suffering and waiting*
> *of speaking alone*
> *to my heart.*

Bite'm wakes up and howls.

"You sing tango better than anyone," says Marko, stepping out of the shadows.

"What do *you* know about tango?" Victoria says, dashing away a tear.

"Shut up, vo. The great Gardel was from Uruguay. We know as much about tango in Uruguay as any Argentine."

Bite'm chases a boy going by on a bicycle. Marko sits

down next to Victoria. "You have to teach that dog how to sing. He's out of tune."

"His voice is better than yours," she says. "What are you doing here?"

"There's a tango that goes, 'One always returns to one's first love.' Do you know it?" he asks.

"Yeah, what of it?"

"I've been looking for you all night."

Victoria looks into his eyes and frowns. "Your eyes are all bloodshot. Stop taking that stuff."

"Sure, sure." He strokes her arm. "Don't get mad."

"I know you sell drugs for the Captain."

Marko gets up to go, but Victoria stops him. "What's that on your shirt? Blood?"

"It's the cops. They beat me up. I'll be okay."

"What happened?"

"I was in the warehouse when the cops burst in. They came for the Captain's drugs, and I was the only one there."

Beto waves and hollers from the café, "We're about to shut down. You better come in now, Victoria!"

"Wait here," Victoria says. She goes over to the storeroom, takes Marko's bucket and returns it to him.

"What's this?" he asks, confused.

"I got another job."

"But I need you at the corner."

"Marko, I can't. I'm sorry." She gives him a hug, but he pushes her away angrily.

"What's going on? What's this new job?"

She hesitates. "I'm gonna sell flowers with Andrés."

"I thought we were friends," Marko says. "More than friends."

"You're always leaving me and going off on your business. I don't want to be involved in any of it." She takes a broom and starts sweeping the sidewalk.

Marko grabs the broom. "Give me the money from today."

"Here," she says, taking it out of her pocket.

Marko takes it and turns to go.

"Hey, where's my share?" Victoria asks, grabbing his arm.

He shakes her off. "You got your flower money . . . and Andrés," he mumbles, turning away.

Victoria goes back to the storeroom, folds an old towel to make a little bed for the puppy and finishes cleaning up.

I have a promise to keep.

CHAPTER NINE

THE NEXT MORNING VICTORIA IS WOKEN UP BY BITE'M licking her cheek. "You could make money working as an alarm clock," she says, scratching his belly. He wiggles in underneath her blanket, and they play hide-and-seek. After getting dressed, Victoria leaves the storeroom to brush her teeth.

Bite'm barks for her.

"Hey!" Moustache shouts. "What's that barking?"

"That's my puppy, Bite'm."

"What's he doing here?"

"His owner was killed. I'm taking care of him. Is that okay?"

"No. I'm sorry," Moustache says, "but you can't keep a dog in a restaurant—it's a health issue."

"He's a good dog. He's trained," she pleads.

"It doesn't matter. You've gotta find another place for that dog."

"I'll do it today," she promises, disappointed. *But where can I take him?*

"You know, I was thinking you should get back into school instead of washing car windows," Moustache says.

"I've got a new job. It's with Andrés, selling flowers at night. I can go to school during the day. It's just that I'm not sure who to talk to." Victoria stops herself from saying anything more. She still hasn't told Moustache or Cacho or Beto about her brothers.

Moustache nods. "You need to go to the school board and speak to them about how to start. It's on the corner of Córdoba and Laprida, in front of Government House."

"Thank you, Moustache. You're the best!" Victoria exclaims. She gives him a kiss on the cheek.

"I know, I know. Now go take that frightening Rottweiler somewhere else."

Victoria hides behind a tree across from her aunt's house.

The wind plays with the worn-out curtains at the windows. She waits a long hour until she sees Juan open the small battered door and leave on his bike. Then she picks up Bite'm and tiptoes inside.

"Who's there?" Doña Norma calls out.

"It's only me," Victoria says, surprised at how sharp the old lady's hearing is. She goes to Betina's room, and is disappointed to find that her brothers and cousin aren't there. There is a new poster on the wall saying that Betina is singing at the Neuquen Club. *The Neuquen!*

Victoria leaves Bite'm on her bed, and goes through the house to check if Aunt Marta is there. Then she goes back to her room and, grabbing a big plastic shopping bag off the dresser, hastily throws her few belongings inside— underwear, shorts, a pair of pants and sandals. She carefully takes the photo of her mother off the wall.

Someone opens the front door. Victoria holds her breath.

"What the hell is going on!" her aunt shouts, bursting into Betina's bedroom. "You have some nerve coming back here after you ran away like that." Her face is red, and the veins on her neck look like they are about to burst.

"I had to leave. You knew what Juan was up to, but you wouldn't listen to me." Victoria pushes past her. "Anyway, I've only come to see Martin and Damian. Where are they?"

"They're with Betina, delivering my sewing."

"Can I wait until they come back? I want to see them."

"No," her aunt snaps. "I want you to get out and stay away from here."

"Don't worry. I'll stay away and I'll take the twins with me as soon as I can."

"Ha! I'd like to see that," Marta says.

Bite'm jumps up and down on the bed barking loudly.

"What is that barking?" Doña Norma calls from her room.

Victoria picks up Bite'm and hurries over to Doña Norma's room.

"Oh! What a cute puppy," the old lady says. She pets his head and he licks her hand. "My Carli was just like him. What's his name?"

"Bite'm," Victoria says.

"That's a funny name." Doña Norma gives a small laugh and coughs. "Ah, little pup, you're so sweet—you make me miss my Carli. I wish I could get a new dog just like you!"

"You should rest, Doña Norma," Marta interrupts. She has been watching from the doorway. "And *you* need to leave," she adds, looking coldly at Victoria.

Victoria kisses Doña Norma goodbye, grabs her plastic bag of clothing and quickly leaves. Bite'm follows her out.

Victoria opens the huge glass door of the school board and walks in, carrying Bite'm and her bag of clothing. She is still shaken from the run-in with her aunt.

A man is sitting at the front desk reading.

"Sir, do you know where I ask about going to school?"

"Upstairs," the man replies, without even looking up from his newspaper. "The elevator is broken."

Victoria walks up the stairs to an office on the second floor with Bite'm trailing behind. A woman is sitting at a desk just inside.

"Are you the person I talk to about going back to school?" Victoria asks, shutting the door behind her.

"Yes, I am," answers the woman, peering over her spectacles. "How old are you?"

"I'm fourteen."

"And what was the last grade you were in?"

"I did a month of grade eight."

"Why did you leave school?"

Victoria takes a deep breath. "My mom died and my father left. I had to go live with my aunt who made me work for her and wouldn't let me go to school."

The woman gives her a concerned look. "You'll have to catch up. You can take the test to see which grade you'll be in at Moreno School next Wednesday, after school gets out. On the 14th. Be there at five o'clock sharp. You'll need to bring an adult with you to sign the papers."

"I live in the back of Los Andes Café. Can the owner come and sign for me?"

"You live in a café?"

"Yes."

"I should contact your aunt."

"Please don't make me go back there!"

The woman shakes her head. "Wait a minute." She dials a number. "Hello, Margarita? This is Claudia from the school board. I have a young girl here who wants to go back to school. She's fourteen and needs a place to live. Do you have anything for her?"

Victoria holds her breath.

"Oh. That's great. Thanks." The woman puts down the phone, scribbles something on a piece of paper and hands it to Victoria. "This lady, Margarita, may have a place for you to live. Go there tomorrow morning, early. She'll give you the things you need for school."

"Thank you so much." Victoria looks at the paper excitedly. *Maybe now things will get a little better.*

She walks out, her steps lighter. Bite'm follows her at a trot, his tail wagging.

Later that afternoon, Victoria returns to her aunt's house. She stops at the corner when she hears the twins laughing. They are playing outside with the boys from next door. "Martin! Damian!"

"Victoria! Victoria!" The boys come running from the neighbour's yard. They jump on Victoria and almost knock her over, kissing and hugging her.

Damian says, "Auntie says you ran away! She says you don't care about us and you're not gonna come back."

"I do care about you. Of course I do. You're the best little brothers in the world."

"Then why don't you come back right now?"

"I've got a better plan. I'm working and pretty soon I'll have enough money for you to come with me."

She sets down her plastic shopping bag.

"What is that?" Damian asks.

"It's moving!" Martin says.

"It's something for you," Victoria says. "Do you want to see what it is?"

The twins nod, jumping up and down with excitement.

Victoria opens the bag and Bite'm leaps out, barking and wagging his tail.

The twins laugh and clap their hands.

"This is Bite'm," Victoria says, smiling.

The puppy dances about, delighted with all the attention.

"Can we really keep him?"

"Yes, but you'll have to feed him and walk him every day. Promise? Betina can help you."

"But Juan doesn't like dogs," Damian says, worriedly.

"I know, but Doña Norma does, and it's her house," Victoria replies. She hugs her two little brothers and says, "Don't worry. Everything will be okay. I love you both so much!" She gives Damian a stick and says, "Here! Bite'm loves to play fetch."

Damian throws the stick and Bite'm leaps after it.

Victoria turns and leaves, wiping away her tears. She doesn't want the boys to see her crying.

MARKO IS WAITING IN FRONT OF THE CAFÉ, LEANING AGAINST a pole with a beer in his hand. He offers the bottle to Victoria. "Here, chiquilina."

She pushes it away, shaking her head. He smiles sheepishly.

"You're all scruffy," she says. "Go back home, Botija. Your mom is waiting for you."

"I'll go if you come with me. Or are you going with Andrés now?"

"I'm not with anybody," Victoria retorts.

"Don't you like me? I want to be with you. I'll stop working with the Captain, if that's what you want. I promise."

"Stop messing with me."

"Really, I swear," he pleads.

"Look, Botija," she says, stepping into the café, "we're still friends."

"But that's not the same." He grabs her arm and the beer spills onto the floor.

"Everything okay?" Moustache asks, coming over. He gives Marko a sharp look.

"Yeah, everything is just great," Marko says, storming off.

A few minutes later, Andrés arrives. "Ready to go?" he asks. He's holding two baskets of flowers. "Let's start with a new place they just opened down there."

At Salta Street, Victoria points to a tall door and says, "That house belongs to Doña Frida. She rents rooms. My mom used to houseclean for her, and I helped."

"Does she know you live in a café?" Andrés asks.

"No," Victoria says. "But it doesn't matter. I could never afford a room there."

AFTER SHE SELLS ALL OF HER FLOWERS, VICTORIA WAITS outside the Flamingo Bar for Andrés.

Marko turns a corner and comes right up to her.

"What are you doing here?" she asks him, flustered.

"Please come back to me."

"No. I already told you."

"Don't get mad, chiquilina." He leans in close to her face and tries to kiss her.

Victoria pushes him away.

Andrés walks out of the club with the flower basket under his arm. "Hey, what's going on here?"

"Nothing's going on, vo," Marko says. "I heard you got a place on Patronato. Good news."

Andrés takes Victoria's arm. "Let's go, muñeca."

"Hey, Maradona!" Marko shouts after him. "Can I have your autograph? I'll sell it when you're famous."

"Sure, whatever," Andrés says, not turning around.

AFTER THEY WALK A FEW BLOCKS, ANDRÉS STOPS AND TURNS to Victoria. "Stay with me tonight."

"I can't. I have to clean up the café."

"I'll help you. It'll be fun. We can go back to my house afterward."

Victoria's heart beats faster. "It's not that I don't want to, but I'm scared."

"Of me?" he asks, taken aback.

"Well, every time I like someone it doesn't work out."

"Don't worry. With me you'll be safe."

"I've heard that before."

He kisses her on the cheek and walks away slowly.

CHAPTER TEN

MARGARITA'S HOUSE IS OLD AND PAINTED GREY. IT HAS double doors, two barred windows and crooked blinds. Victoria knocks and waits anxiously.

I'll have my own bed, she thinks. *And I'll finally get to go to school.*

A short woman with long black hair opens the door. "Can I help you?"

"Are you Margarita?" Victoria asks hopefully.

"Yes, my dear. And you must be Victoria. I've been expecting you. Claudia, the lady at the school board, told me all about you."

She has a nice smile.

Margarita ushers Victoria into the house. "Follow me to the kitchen. I bet you're hungry. Have you had breakfast yet?" Without waiting for an answer, Margarita brings out a plate of sliced bread and jam. "Tell me about yourself, m'hija."

"Well, I'm living at Los Andes Café," Victoria says between mouthfuls. "The owner lets me sleep in the storeroom, and I clean up for him. And I also sell flowers at night in the bars."

Margarita gives her a cup of *mate cocido*. "You can sleep here. A girl left two days ago, so I've got space. I found a family in Buenos Aires that hired her as a nanny."

"Thank you, Doña, you're so kind. I can help out here— I'm a good cook, and I know how to wash and sew."

"There's always something to do. Wait here," Margarita says, going out to the patio.

Victoria looks around the room, feeling safe and relieved to be somewhere she is welcome.

Margarita returns carrying a plastic bag and some sheets. Putting the bag on the table, she says, "Here are some school supplies you'll need."

"These make me feel like starting school right away," Victoria says, rummaging through the bag excitedly.

"Claudia told me about the placement test. I can be at Moreno School to sign for you on the 14th," says Margarita with a smile. "Now why don't you finish your breakfast while I make your bed."

Victoria sips her drink gratefully and listens to the radio. "Here's a request by Marco Antonio, who dedicates the tango 'Uno', by Discépolo and Mores, to his girlfriend Maria Victoria."

Victoria chokes.

The first notes of the song begin, but the announcer keeps talking. Finally, he stops and she listens.

Full of hope, you seek
the pathway to the dreams
you promised yourself.
You know that the struggle will be cruel and long,
but you'll fight and you'll bleed
for this stubbornly held faith.

"It's amazing how many people phone in to pay homage to Don Enrique Santos Discépolo on this special show about his life and music. And now we have a call from . . . just a second, I can't read our new receptionist's handwriting. Che, Roxanna, come and tell me what the hell you have written here, because this looks like Chinese."

"Che, Fatso, stop. We're on the air," a woman's voice yells back.

Victoria laughs.

Margarita walks back into the kitchen. "I'll wash the dishes," she says, going over to the sink. "Can you dry them?"

"Sure," Victoria answers.

"Now we are going to play 'Hoodlums', by Discépolo and Filiberto, requested by Omar Cos, a faithful listener from Victoria City."

Tell me, by God, what have you done to me!
That I've changed so much,
I don't know who I am anymore . . .
Don't you see, I'm suffocated,
defeated and hobbled,
in your heart.
I saw myself in jail or dead . . .

When the drying is done, Victoria puts down her dishtowel and sits on a chair with her elbows on the table. The fingers of her right hand trace the pattern of the sky-blue tablecloth. *I wonder what Marko is going to do. I hope he stays out of trouble.*

Margarita's voice shakes Victoria out of her daydream. "Come with me. I'll show you which drawer you can put your clothes in and where the key is kept."

Victoria follows her outside and through a patio at the back of the house. It is littered with bricks and bags of cement.

"Be careful," Margarita says. "Emilio never cleans up after his work. He's building a little washroom here."

On the other side of the patio, there are two white doors with small windows on either side.

"That's the boys' room and this one is the girls'," Margarita says.

The girls' room has four bunk beds, and a chest of

drawers with an oval mirror on the top. The walls are full of TV stars' photos.

"Some of the girls are at school and others are at work," Margarita says, pointing at a bed. "This will be yours. Just bring your stuff whenever you'd like. Here's a key."

"Thank you for everything, Doña."

NEAR THE PLAZA, SOMEONE CATCHES VICTORIA'S EYE. *It's Chichón. She's limping!*

"What happened?" Victoria asks, running to her.

"It's my uncle. He beat me again." Chichón lifts her t-shirt gingerly and turns around. Her back is covered with bruises.

Victoria gasps. "You can't ever go back."

"I'm not going to," Chichón says. "I don't care what happens."

"I have an idea. Come with me." Victoria gently takes her arm and leads her down the street.

"Where are we going?"

"You can take my place at the café until you go to the bakery in Rosario."

Chichón sighs. "I don't think that's ever gonna happen."

"Don't give up," Victoria says. "And the guys at the café are good people—they can keep an eye out for you."

After talking with Moustache and settling Chichón in at the café, Victoria goes over to see Andrés at the newsstand. She tells him about her new home and starting school.

"That's great, muñeca. Let's celebrate tonight," Andrés says, smiling.

"My cousin, Betina, is singing at the Neuquen. We could go there."

"That'll be cool. We can sell flowers there."

"Great."

Two giant posters of Betina cover the pillars of the main entrance to the Neuquen Club. There's a big Friday night crowd lined up at the front door.

After she sells her flowers, Victoria grabs Andrés and they go up to the doorman. "I'm Betina's cousin."

"Go round the back. She's getting ready to sing," the man says.

They walk in and find Betina putting on her makeup. Her dark hair has copper highlights, and she's wearing a bright red blouse, mini-skirt and black boots.

"Hello, sweetheart!" Betina exclaims. "Where have you been? I've been worried sick." She hugs Victoria tightly. "I don't blame you for running away. Are you alright? Do you need anything?"

"No, it's okay. I've got a place to stay. And I've been selling flowers with Andrés," she says, pulling him forward. He smiles and hands Betina a bouquet.

"Thank you!" she says.

"And I'm going to start school soon," Victoria adds.

"That's great! I'm so happy for you," Betina says and kisses her cousin.

"How are the twins?"

"They're fine. They love the puppy and so does Doña Norma. That was a good thing you did."

"I'm so glad," Victoria says, smiling.

"We'll cheer for you," Andrés says.

Betina smiles. "You better. Meet me at the bar after the show."

THE VOICE OF THE MC BOOMS. HE'S A YOUNG MAN WEARING black pants, a white shirt and a red bow tie. He talks nonsense for a while and then, making a grand sweeping gesture, he introduces: "BETIIIIINAAAAAAAAA!!!!"

The audience leaps to its feet and applauds wildly.

Betina takes the stage and begins her first song. For a moment, the audience quiets, then they cheer and whistle their appreciation. Betina sings ten cumbias without a break. The audience begs for more, calling her name and reaching out to touch her. Two bulky men on either side of the stage push away anyone who tries to clamber onto it.

Betina takes her bows and vanishes behind the curtain, but the shouts and whistles continue.

"She's amazing," Andrés says to Victoria when they get to the bar.

"I know." She nods, happy for her cousin, happy to be enjoying this moment with Andrés. They find a couple of empty stools and sit down.

They aren't the only ones awaiting the star of the evening. Fans at the bar jump to their feet when Betina arrives. They demand autographs, congratulate her and take pictures. When she breaks free, she gestures for Victoria and Andrés to join her at a table.

"What did you think of the show?" Betina asks.

"It was fantastic," Andrés says.

An older man with a thin moustache, holding a whiskey, comes to the table and says, "You were great, mamita."

"Thanks, Ramón," Betina says, giving him a kiss. She turns to Victoria. "I have a gift for you at home."

"Oh, thanks Beti. Why don't we meet tomorrow at Alvear Plaza?"

"Sure. How about noon? I'll try to bring the twins."

"Yes, please."

Ramón puts his hand on Betina's shoulder. "We have to go now." They get up and leave.

"That guy with Betina is the manager here," Andrés says.

"I guess so . . ."

They get up to dance, and Victoria pulls Andrés close.

"You're a really good dancer," she says.

"You should see my moves on the soccer field!" He laughs.

When they leave, a boy on the sidewalk selling *choripán* sees Andrés and sings:

> Buy her a choripán, buy her a choripán
>
> the skinny girl is hungry, buy her a choripán.

"Che, Pocho the Panther, give me those two really well-done ones—there in the back," Andrés says.

The boy hands them their snack, and they stroll down the street, eating and talking about the show.

"How about coming home with me tonight?" Andrés asks, slipping his hand around her waist.

Victoria looks up at him and spots the smile he is hiding. "Okay," she says and kisses him.

A LOW WALL FRAMES THE GARDEN AROUND THE LITTLE white house where Andrés lives. He opens a door, and they enter a small green kitchen. A single bulb, hanging from the centre of the ceiling, illuminates the room. There's a wooden table against the wall with a trophy on a shelf above it—*Winged Victory*, a shining golden woman, about twenty centimeters tall, with open wings.

"That's my other *Victoria Alada*," Andrés says.

Victoria smiles shyly.

A few magazines and old newspapers are on the table, and a pile of dishes and glasses lie upside down on a draining board.

"I like it here," she says.

"I should repaint it. I'm tired of the green walls," Andrés says.

Victoria laughs nervously.

Opening the fridge, he asks, "What do you want to drink? I have a bottle of cold water or . . . nothing else."

"I like cold water more than nothing else."

He laughs and takes out the bottle and invites her into the living room. There is a brown leatherette sofa, with blankets, a pillow and a sheet. The wall is papered with pictures of soccer players torn from sports magazines and pictures of motorcycles cut from old calendars.

A deep snore rumbles from behind a half-closed door.

"That's my father. He sleeps like a log," Andrés says. Then he sits on the couch and pats the cushion. Victoria sinks down next to him.

"Is your mother asleep too?" she asks.

"She left for Buenos Aires five years ago."

"Why?"

"She was supposed to find a job, and then we'd join her."

"What happened?"

"First, she sent us letters telling us to delay our trip.

Then she told us not to come, that she wanted to live there without us," Andrés says, lowering his voice. "I think she found someone else."

"I'm really sorry. That must be awful."

Andrés puts his arm around her. "Don't feel sorry. We're surviving," he says. "And enough of that serious stuff—tomorrow's my birthday."

"Oh, it's your birthday? You didn't tell me!"

"Well, you didn't ask."

"Let's do something special tomorrow. What do you want to do?"

"I was thinking of going fishing. I love fishing."

"Me too." Victoria smiles. "When I was a little girl, my father used to take me out on the river. We'd spend the whole afternoon pulling out catfish. He was so different then."

They pass the bottle of water back and forth, sharing more stories. When the bottle is empty, Andrés sets it down and gently pushes the hair away from Victoria's face. "You're so beautiful," he says. He leans over and kisses her.

"It's late . . ." Victoria says.

Andrés smiles. "I know. You can have the sofa, I'll sleep in my dad's room."

For the first time in a long time, Victoria feels safe. "Thank you, Andrés."

He kisses her again. "Goodnight, muñeca."

CHAPTER ELEVEN

Victoria wakes up and sees a pale orange light. *It's already morning.* She looks around and listens. She can't see anyone, but she can hear snores from the next room.

She dresses quickly and goes outside.

An early morning breeze carries the scent of jasmine from vines covering a trellis. Victoria breathes it in.

A moment later, Andrés pulls up on Gringo's motorbike. "Good morning, muñeca!" he says, smiling. He's carrying a leather newspaper bag.

"Happy birthday!" Victoria kisses him.

Andrés tucks Victoria's hair behind her ear. "We'll go fishing after my football practice. I'll pick up a couple of rods and meet you at the newsstand around two, okay?"

"Sounds good," she says, smiling.

As Victoria crosses Alvear Plaza, Marko comes up and surprises her. "I have some news for you, chiquilina."

"You again!" she exclaims.

"Chill. Please, just hear me out. That boy you were worried about—the one with the scar. He's dead. He was killed last night in a fight."

"Wow," Victoria gasps. "I guess it's no surprise."

"And another thing," he says, sitting down on a bench. "I'm leaving soon for Montevideo."

"Your mother will be happy," Victoria says.

She sits down next to him.

"Yeah. And I'm going to make some good money—enough to help her set up a flower stall."

"And how are you going to do that?"

"I just take a little something to Punta del Este—where the fat cats go. It's not far from Montevideo."

"So you're still licking the Captain's boots. It will end badly . . . you know that."

"Don't worry. I'll be fine. It'll be my last job for him. Why don't you come with me?"

"You must be joking."

"No, I mean it."

Victoria ignores this. "How are you going to get there?"

"By bus to Concordia, then a guy will take me by boat to the other side. I'm leaving on Thursday morning." He takes a bus ticket from his bag and shows it to her.

"Be careful, okay?"

He takes her hand. "There's still time to change your mind."

Victoria shakes her head.

"Give me another chance," he says.

"No." She pulls her hand away.

"One day I'm going to come back for you," Marko says, his voice cracking. "I'll come back and take you to Montevideo with me. You'll see the beach, the walkway, the old town, the market. I'll show you where the *candomberos* call out."

"Sounds nice there."

"Can I see you one more time before I leave?"

"Maybe. I'll be around."

The Captain's fluorescent green motorcycle screeches to a stop in front of them. Marko hurriedly hops on and it speeds off, zigzagging between cars.

When Victoria opens the door to the café, Beto asks, "Is everything okay?"

"Yeah, sure."

"So when do you start school?"

"Next week," Victoria says. "I've come to get my stuff. Has Chichón been working out?"

"Yes," he says. "But he's still in the back room."

Victoria goes to the storeroom door, knocks lightly and opens it. "Hey, Chichón, what's wrong? I told you, after breakfast you need to be out of here until close-up time."

Chichón gets up, stuffing her hair under a cap. "I'm afraid to hang out on the streets. If my uncle sees me, he'll kill me."

"I have an idea." Victoria takes a deep breath. "Come with me and meet Margarita. You can help her during the day—there's lots to do there. She'll like you. And you won't have to pretend to be a boy there."

"Do you really think so?"

"I do. Let's go, now."

AFTER VICTORIA INTRODUCES CHICHÓN TO MARGARITA, she hurries over to Alvear Plaza to meet her cousin.

She hopes Betina will have the twins, but her cousin is sitting by herself.

"I thought you were bringing the twins," Victoria says.

"I tried, I promise, but my mom wouldn't let me bring them. But, look, I have something for you. It's for school." She hands Victoria a package wrapped in bright blue paper held together with gold ribbon tied in a giant bow.

"Thank you, Beti."

"It's nothing."

Victoria pulls the ribbon off. Despite her disappointment about her brothers, her eyes light up. It's a white pinafore with buttons up the front. She holds it out, admiring it.

"It was my *guardapolvo*," Betina says. "I've been saving it for you all these years."

"It's lovely!" Victoria gives Betina a hug.

"It's the first step. When you become a teacher, I'll buy you a new one."

Victoria smiles at her cousin with gratitude. "It's really going to happen. I know it," she says. "Now tell me about the twins. Is Aunt Marta treating them okay?"

"They're fine."

"One day they're going to come and live with me," she says.

"I know you'll do it. I'll try to help you, believe me."

"Are they looking after Bite'm?"

"They love him. So does Doña Norma."

"How are things going with that boyfriend of yours?"

"He's a son of a bitch."

"Really!"

"He's messing around with another girl. Last night he told me he doesn't want me singing at the Neuquen anymore."

"That's awful, but you're better off without him."

"Yeah, but now I have to find another place to sing. I was thinking maybe I should go to Buenos Aires. People say I should, but I'm not sure about it."

Victoria takes Betina's hand and squeezes it. "Che, Beti, Andrés knows all the bar owners here. He'll help you find another place to sing, I'm sure."

"Do you really think so?"

"Yeah, don't worry. I'll tell him to ask around."

Betina looks relieved. "I love you so much," she says, hugging Victoria. "You know that, right?"

"Yeah, I know that. I love you too. Meet me here tomorrow afternoon, and I'll tell you what Andrés comes up with."

Betina nods. "I will. At the same time?"

"Sure. Thanks for the present. Give the twins a kiss for me and try to bring them with you tomorrow."

AFTER BETINA LEAVES, VICTORIA GOES TO THE KIOSK TO wait for Andrés. She hands the package to Gringo. "Can you put this away for me, che? It's my school uniform. I'm starting soon."

"That's great, Victoria. No problem, I'll look after it," he says and points down the road. "Look, the birthday boy's coming."

Andrés pulls up on Gringo's motorcycle. He hops off and parks the bike next to the stand, smiling at Victoria. There are two fishing rods tied onto the back of the bike. Andrés hands Victoria one. "It's a little rusty, but it still works just fine."

"Thanks, che," Victoria says, taking the fishing rod from

him. "You missed seeing my cousin Betina. She gave me her old school uniform."

"It's my birthday, and you're the one who gets a present!"

"Listen, Andrés. She lost her job and she's worried that she won't be able to find another one. Maybe one of the bars has a spot for her. Can you ask around?"

"Sure, why not? Come on, let's go before the mosquitoes come out."

Holding hands in the warm sun, they walk to Urquiza Park. They wind their way through the ravine, walking along the low stone wall, until they reach an open stretch of riverbank.

Andrés squelches through the mud and turns over a big rock. "Look, worms!" He scoops up a few and drops them into a plastic bag he has brought. Then he and Victoria take their time collecting more worms for bait, digging their hands into the damp earth, feeling the fresh mud between their fingers.

Victoria smiles as the little creatures wriggle in the palms of her hands. "They tickle," she laughs.

"Here's another one!" Marko comes up from behind, slipping a worm down Andrés' back.

Andrés shouts and shakes out his shirt. "What are you doing? Get lost, *pendejo*!"

"So you guys are going fishing?" Marko asks. "I'll join you."

"We only have two fishing rods," Andrés says.

"That's okay. I can catch a fish with my bare hands."

"Yeah, and I can jump across the river in one leap."

Victoria interrupts, "Andrés, Marko's leaving for Uruguay next week."

"I won't miss him," Andrés says.

"But I will. And he was there for me when I needed help. Let's not fight with him."

ALL ALONG THE RIVER, GROUPS OF PEOPLE ENJOY THEIR DAY off, singing and dancing, drinking mate and beer, laughing and playing loud music.

When I ran away, I was sick and frightened. Today I am fishing with my friends. Mamá, please stay with me as I try to find my way.

Victoria, Andrés and Marko walk until they find a quiet spot—a small bay, surrounded by willows and *palos borrachos*. They settle down in the shade to fish. Andrés and Victoria throw their baited hooks into the brown water and wait. They talk softly, not wanting to startle the fish—their eyes fixed on the corks rolling in the water. Every so often the corks dip beneath the surface, and they pull in a tiny catfish, only to throw it back into the river.

"The only things biting here are the mosquitoes," Marko says, slapping his arm. He ventures over onto a half-submerged wharf. "Hey, look!" he shouts.

"What is it?" Andrés shouts back.

"It's an old boat," Marko says. It wobbles as he climbs in.

"You're going to tip over, idiot!" Victoria shouts. "That boat's more dangerous than a drunken barber."

"Come on! Don't be scared," Marko yells. "There's bound to be better fishing in the middle of the river. Don't be a baby."

"He's right for the first time. We won't catch anything here," Andrés says to Victoria. "Okay, we're coming," he shouts to Marko, pulling in his line and going over to the wharf.

Victoria follows and soon all three of them are sitting precariously in the boat.

Andrés passes his rod to Marko and takes the two old oars. "There's something under the seat," he says. Surprised, he pulls out a box of wine. "Look at this! And it's full." He takes off the cap, swallows a mouthful of wine and wipes his mouth with the back of his hand. He hands the wine to Victoria.

She shakes her head. "I hate wine."

Marko grabs the box from Andrés and sings a cumbia:

Look at how vulgar I am, look at how vulgar I am;
I drink cheap wine from a box,

I drink cheap wine from a box.

And when I get too drunk, and when I get too drunk;

I feel like running wild, I feel like running wild.

"Che, you're a mosquito, Botija," says Andrés.

"Why, vo?"

"You suck."

Laughing, the two boys drink the wine and sing "Happy Birthday."

Victoria is quiet, enjoying her friends' antics, cradled by the gentle rocking of the river.

All of a sudden, Marko's rod bends into an arc. "Aaaay!" he shouts. "It's a big one!"

Andrés steadies the dinghy with the oars and Marko, struggling with the line, pulls in an enormous fish. It's a beautiful *surubí*. "This must weigh two kilos!" he shouts excitedly. He takes the fish off the hook, and it writhes on the bottom of the boat. Marko stands up and shouts at the people on the riverbank. "I caught the biggest fish in the world!"

"Sit down!" Victoria shrieks, laughing.

A speed boat startles them. It swooshes by and a large wave slaps the boat, rocking it back and forth violently. Victoria holds on tightly. Marko stumbles, flails his arms wildly and falls backward into the river. His black and yellow cap floats to the surface.

Victoria screams, "He's drowning! Do something, quick!"

Andrés dives into the river next to the hat and disappears.

"Be careful!" she shouts after him.

It feels like an eternity until Andrés breaks the surface, gasping for air. He's holding Marko by the collar. He pulls him to the boat. Victoria grabs Marko's arm and tugs, while Andrés heaves him over the side. Andrés climbs in after him, spluttering. Marko lies in the bottom of the boat, coughing and spitting water.

"Are you alright?" Victoria asks.

Marko coughs again and nods.

"We'd better get back straight away," Victoria says, reaching into the water for Marko's cap.

Andrés rows hard, but they make slow headway. Finally they reach shore and help Marko onto the floating dock.

They walk back to the city in silence.

"Hey, Andrés. Thanks, vo," Marko says.

"I did it for Victoria," Andrés replies, handing him the bag with the fish. "What are you going to do with it?"

"You keep it," Marko says.

"Okay, let's cook it at my house."

Victoria sings.

> *We friends were always three*
> *in the days of our youth . . .*
> *We were the most-talked about trio*
> *that has ever walked*
> *these southern streets . . .*

CHAPTER TWELVE

CHURCH BELLS ARE RINGING LOUDLY AS VICTORIA GETS TO the kiosk. At the corner, two boys she hasn't seen before are washing car windows.

Gringo is behind the counter drinking mate and helping a customer. He takes a copy of *Ábrete seso* off the shelf.

"It's for my granddaughter," the customer says, taking the magazine from Gringo and handing him some coins. "She loves the stories and games in it."

Just then, Andrés rides up. He's wearing a red and black Patronato jersey.

Victoria takes an elastic band from the counter and pulls her hair into a ponytail. "Hey Andrés, did you talk to anyone about Betina?"

"Yeah, she has to go to the bar at Vodebil and ask for

the owner. He'll be expecting her tonight." He cuts the string binding a bundle of magazines with a knife. "Mission accomplished."

"Great," Victoria says, smiling. "Thanks, che." She gives Andrés a kiss on the cheek and starts helping him set up.

"You're good at this," Gringo remarks. "Can you help Andrés while I run an errand?"

"Sure," Victoria says, pleased. Gringo walks off in the direction of Los Andes.

Victoria hands a copy of *Para tí* to a woman. Andrés taps her on the shoulder, pointing. "Look who's coming."

Betina and the twins walk up to the kiosk with Bite'm trotting behind. Victoria runs around to the front and hugs them all. *Mamá would be so happy to see us together on a Sunday afternoon.*

As Betina and Victoria talk, the puppy sniffs trees and barks at pigeons while the twins chase him.

"Andrés talked to the owner of Vodebil," Victoria tells her cousin. "He says to meet him at the bar tonight before the show."

"Great! Thanks, Andrés!" Betina exclaims, a smile spreading across her face.

"Anything to help Victoria's cousin."

The roar of an engine interrupts them. A motorcycle pulls up, the Captain jumps off the back and the motorbike speeds away. "Che, *pendeja*!"

Victoria pushes the twins behind her. Andrés steps out of the stand.

"Where's Marko?" the Captain barks at Victoria.

"You should know," she says.

Spitting on the sidewalk, the Captain takes out a gun and points it at Andrés. "What do you think you're gonna do with that knife, *pelotudo*?"

Bite'm snarls. With a worried look at Victoria, Betina takes the twins by the hand and leads them away. The puppy follows.

"We're wasting time here," the Captain says.

"The last time we saw Marko was yesterday. We don't know where he is now," Victoria says, her voice trembling.

Andrés puts his knife away and steps in front of Victoria. "Try Bambino's. He always goes there."

"You better be right," the Captain says, walking over to Gringo's bike. "Is Chichón around?"

"Maybe he's with Cogote," Victoria says.

The Captain ignores her. He runs his hand along the bike's leather seat. "Nice bike." He puts his gun in his waistband, slowly turns around and walks to the corner where the new squeegee boys are at work.

"I told you not to get mixed up with Marko," Andrés says.

"I'm not . . . anymore. We'd better warn Chichón."

"I'll look for him. You go find Betina and the twins and have fun. It's a beautiful day."

"Thanks, che. See you later." She kisses him before running to join her brothers and her cousin.

The twins are throwing a stick for Bite'm to fetch.

"Who was that guy? Do you know him?" Betina asks.

"The Captain. He's bad news."

They go down Córdoba Street toward the river and amble up the wide pathways.

"I'm hungry!" Damian says, tugging at Victoria's sleeve. "I want an ice cream."

"I want a hot dog!" Martin shouts. He points to a stand close by.

"Okay," Betina says. "My treat."

The stand has a sign on it that says HOTDONALD's. As the man takes their order, he recognizes Betina and greets her nervously. "I saw you at the Neuquen. You were fantastic," he says, handing her a hot dog. "The guys aren't going to believe me when I tell them I sold you a hot dog."

Betina smiles modestly and thanks him.

A group of musicians are playing on the grass, surrounded by a small crowd. Nearby, there is a group of dogs, feasting on leftovers dropped on the ground. Bite'm joins them.

A man playing a guitar waves to Betina. "Come here, Beti! Let's have a song!"

"Oh! That's Chelo. He's in the first band I ever sang with." Betina makes her way over and squeezes in between the musicians. They perform one, two, three cumbias.

"Bravo! *Otra*! *Otra*!" the crowd shouts, ecstatic. The hotdog man elbows his way through to Betina, hands her a slip of paper and a pen and pleads, "Please, madam, can I have your autograph?"

Betina signs with a smile and adds a lipstick kiss to the paper. "There you are."

He blushes and quickly returns with two cans of pop.

"I want the Pepsi," Martin pipes up.

"I want the Oh-range," says Damian.

"Orange. It's just one word. ORANGE," Victoria says. "And say 'thank you' to the man."

After the twins gulp down their drinks, they run to the top of a little hill and disappear from sight. Betina and Victoria sit under an *espinillo* full of yellow flowers. Victoria picks one from a low-hanging, heavily-laden branch, smells it and sighs. "Mamá loved espinillo. She used to take small branches and put them in a vase I made for her at school out of a cut-up plastic bottle."

Martin reappears at the top of the hill, bolts down it and parks himself on Victoria's lap. "Victoria, when is Papa coming back? Auntie says that he isn't coming back ever."

Struggling for the right words, Victoria hesitates before saying, "You shouldn't listen to her."

"Hello, Victoria," a voice says.

Victoria looks over her shoulder. "Doña Frida!" she exclaims.

"Are these your brothers?" Doña Frida smiles at the two little boys.

"Yes. This is Martin and this is Damian. Give Doña Frida a kiss," Victoria says, pushing the twins toward her.

Betina gets up. "Oh, Doña Frida, my aunt spoke so highly of you," she says. "I'm Betina, Victoria's cousin."

"I watched you singing just now. You have a wonderful voice, my dear. You remind me of Gladys, *la bomba tucumana*."

"Thank you. I sing in the clubs."

Doña Frida turns to Victoria. "Now, dear, tell me what's been going on. My daughter Marcia said she saw you washing car windows near San Miguel Church. Is that true?"

Victoria feels a sense of dread. *I'd better tell her the truth.* "Well, yes, Doña Frida. I couldn't live at my aunt's anymore."

"I see. Where do you live now?"

"I'm staying at a lady's house. She takes kids in and helps them out."

"And what about you, Betina?"

"I'm saving up to get my own place."

Victoria cuts in. "Doña Frida has a boarding house. She might have a room for rent."

"As a matter of fact, I might," Doña Frida says. "Why don't you come to my place and have a look?"

THE TALL DOOR OF DOÑA FRIDA'S HOUSE IS OPEN. A YOUNG lady is sweeping the passage. She hums to the rhythm of a tune coming from a small radio set on a window sill.

Doña Frida greets her, "Hi Marilén." Victoria and Betina also say hello, and the two little boys introduce Bite'm. Then they all follow Doña Frida inside like ducks in a row.

I remember helping Mamá sweep the hall and polish the floors.

Doña Frida briskly leads them to the kitchen. "Why don't I make you a snack? Little boys are always hungry." Doña Frida points to a light blue door. "Go wash your hands in the washroom down the hallway."

"Martin, Damian, you go with Betina. I'll help here," Victoria says. She washes her hands in the kitchen sink, cleans the table with a wet towel and washes the dishes from the lodgers' breakfast.

"You remind me of your mother," Doña Frida says, as she fills a basket with cookies. "You have her beautiful eyes and her kindness."

When Betina and the twins return, Doña Frida pours a cup of chocolate milk for everyone and puts some leftover meatballs in a dish for Bite'm. He devours them under the table. The twins finish their cookies and wrestle with Bite'm on the kitchen floor.

"Now come up with me, and I'll show you the room," Doña Frida says. She leads Victoria and Betina upstairs to a long hallway and opens the door to a small room. The girls get a whiff of wax and see a shining wooden floor, a bed with a carved headboard and and a bright blue blanket.

"It's half the size of the other rooms," Doña Frida says, "so the rent is very little."

"I love the room," Betina says. "Can I get back to you tomorrow about possibly renting it?"

"Of course," Doña Frida says, smiling. "I'd like you to live here. Then perhaps I'll see Victoria and her brothers more often."

"I NEED TO GET READY TO MEET THE GUY AT VODEBIL." Betina says. "I'd better hurry." She and the twins say goodbye to Victoria at the corner.

"Good luck! I'm sure you'll get the job." Victoria gives Betina an encouraging squeeze.

"If I do, I can move into Doña Frida's."

Victoria hugs the twins and watches as they walk away hand in hand with Betina.

CHAPTER THIRTEEN

On Wednesday, Victoria wakes up filled with anticipation. She touches the photo she has taped to the wall beside her bed. *I hope I do well on the test, Mamá.*

While she is doing dishes in the kitchen, her daydreams are interrupted by a loud knocking. Marko is at the door, clutching his arm. It's bleeding. He has a grim look on his face.

"What happened? Are you okay?" Victoria helps him into the kitchen. "I'll get Margarita."

"No, don't!" Marko exclaims. "I don't want more trouble."

Victoria grabs a towel and presses it against Marko's arm to stop the bleeding. "Tell me what happened."

"The Captain," he mumbles through gritted teeth. "He stole Gringo's motorcycle. Andrés and I tried to stop him."

Victoria freezes. "Is Andrés okay?"

"The Captain laid into him worse than me." Marko avoids her eyes.

"Where is he?" Victoria asks, alarmed.

"An ambulance took him to San Martin Hospital."

"Why didn't you go too? You're bleeding!"

"It's slowing down. It's not as bad as it looks."

"If the Captain wasn't looking for you," Victoria says, angrily, "none of this would have happened."

"I'll fix things, I promise."

AT THE HOSPITAL, A YOUNG RECEPTIONIST IS TRYING TO KEEP things under control. Dozens of people are asking questions.

Victoria makes her way down long corridors and follows the signs to the emergency ward.

It's chaos. An old woman is praying, children are crying and young men with fractures, cuts and burns line the wall. There isn't a doctor or nurse in sight.

Victoria looks around, but can't find Andrés. *Where is he?* Panicked, she rushes back the way she came, peering into each room along the way.

There are even more people in front of the reception desk. Victoria slips through the crowd and touches the receptionist's arm. "I'm looking for Andrés Peralta," she says.

"Go to the back of the line and wait like everyone else."

"Andrés Peralta," she insists. "An ambulance brought him in."

"There are other people here with problems besides you."

All of a sudden, a TV reporter shoves a microphone at the receptionist. "What's your opinion about the workers' strike at San Martin?"

"What?" the receptionist asks, bewildered.

"Could you tell our viewers what's happening here today, señorita?"

"Well, as you can see, it's chaos," the woman says, frowning into the camera.

Now is my chance. Victoria quickly ducks behind the desk and scoops up the registry book, scanning it for Andrés' name. *Nothing.*

She searches frantically for Andrés, walking up and down the hallway, dodging people, stretchers, dogs and oxygen tanks. *He must be here somewhere.* Finally she sees him. He's asleep on a folding bed inside a room with other patients. A yellowing sheet covers him up to his chest. His face is swollen; there's a deep gash across his right eyebrow and dried blood on his neck. He has a bandage covering his head and his arm is in a sling. *Oh my God.*

A man in the next bed sits up and says, "That kid really took a beating."

Victoria sits down on the chair beside Andrés' bed.

"I'm so sorry. You were right about Marko," she whispers, reaching out and stroking his hair. She lowers her head onto the edge of the bed and closes her eyes tightly. Taking his hand in hers, she thinks she feels a weak squeeze in return.

Victoria blinks in the bright beam of sunlight and realizes she has fallen asleep. A young nurse comes in with a tray and sets it down. "Lunch!"

Andrés opens his eyes.

"You're awake," Victoria says, taking his hand. "How are you feeling?"

"Terrible," he croaks, smiling weakly.

"Do you want me to tell the cops about what happened?"

"No!" he says fiercely, his face creased with pain. He lowers his voice. "The Captain will get us. Besides, the police don't care."

He's right. Victoria takes the tray to his bed. They share mate cocido and biscuits.

Another nurse comes into the room. "How are you feeling, young man? Someone will be here shortly to take you to have your arm set and a cast put on."

A look of dismay crosses Andrés' face. Victoria knows what he must be thinking.

The nurse writes something down on the chart and leaves.

"No soccer for a while." Andrés looks up at the ceiling.

"Don't worry, che. You'll be scoring goals sooner than you think."

Orderlies arrive, pushing a gurney. On the count of three, they heave Andrés onto it. He winces, but smiles at Victoria as they wheel him away.

Victoria is looking out the window when Gringo arrives with a couple of magazines in his hand. "Where's Andrés?" he asks.

"They're putting a cast on his arm."

"Tell him I came by, and that he shouldn't worry about the newsstand. I'll deliver the morning papers and tell his father what happened."

"What about your bike?"

"Don't worry about that. It doesn't matter. Andrés will be okay, that's the important thing. I'll borrow a bike from my brother for now." Gringo hands her the magazines before leaving. "These are for Andrés. All the latest soccer news."

When Andrés is brought back, gauze covers the stitches across his eyebrow. There are orange splotches on the bandages from the antiseptic.

He looks groggy, but listens as Victoria tells him about Gringo's visit.

Betina comes into the room in her high heels.

"Hello Andrés," she says, looking concerned. "I went to the newsstand and Gringo told me about what happened. How are you doing?" She gives Victoria a kiss.

"His arm was broken," Victoria says. "He won't be able to play with his team for a while, but he'll be alright."

"I'll be fine," Andrés says, with a weak smile.

"I have some good news," Betina says.

"About Vodebil?"

"Yes. I sang and they want me to start on Friday. And you know what?"

"What?"

Betina smiles.

"Go on, tell us," Victoria urges her.

"One of the guys from the Angosta Band was there, and he invited me for a drink and said they were looking for a female voice for their group."

"And?"

"I'm going over to rehearse with them right now!"

"I knew it. You're going to be famous!" Andrés says.

"And it's all because of you," Betina says, beaming at Andrés.

"I take the test for starting school at five o'clock today." Victoria says.

"Good luck," Betina says.

Then she gives them both a kiss and rushes out.

VICTORIA STANDS IN THE HALLWAY OF MORENO SCHOOL looking for the office. There's a lot of confusion with kids gathering in groups, talking and goofing around before they go home.

Victoria stops a young girl. "Can you show me where the office is, please?"

"Down there," the girl says, pointing.

The room has a cardboard sign stuck to the glass that says OFFICE. Victoria walks in nervously. A lady behind the desk looks up.

"Hi, I'm Victoria Diaz."

"You're here for the placement test, right?" the woman asks, looking at a list.

"Yes, I am."

"Come with me. Everyone else is there already." She ushers Victoria into a nearby classroom.

Victoria finds an empty desk and sits down. It's covered with messages that have been carved by students over the years. She traces one with her finger. *Good luck!*

A girl with blonde hair gathered into a long braid is sitting at the next desk. She smiles at Victoria. The boy sitting behind the girl with the braid catches Victoria's eye. She gasps audibly. *It's the other boy! He was with the boy with the scar.*

He leans across and whispers to her, "Don't be frightened. I've left the gang. I never wanted that kind of life."

Victoria nods. "I heard what happened to your friend."

"He wasn't my friend," the boy replies. "Don't tell anyone about what happened, okay?"

"I don't know what you're talking about. I've never seen you before in my life."

A teacher with a stack of tests enters the room and hands them out. "In an hour we will collect the test. If you finish earlier, hand it in. Do your best."

The test is hard, but Victoria tries to answer everything, guessing at some of the questions.

MARGARITA IS IN THE HALLWAY WHEN SHE LEAVES THE classroom. "How did it go, Victoria?"

"Not too bad. I answered all the questions anyway."

"That's good. I've taken care of your registration. You'll start school next week."

Victoria is ecstatic, but she sees that Margarita's face is serious. "I'm afraid I've got some bad news. Chichón's uncle came by and dragged her away with him. I couldn't do anything to stop him. Before he left, he threatened to kill me if I ever took her back."

Poor Chichón. What's going to happen to her now?

VICTORIA GOES TO THE CAFÉ AND GREETS MOUSTACHE. "Chichón won't be coming in for a while," she tells him.

"Actually, he . . . she's in the store-room."

Victoria is taken aback. "You know she's a girl?"

"Someone beat her and I bandaged her face," Moustache says. "That's when I found out. I think you should go back there. She won't tell me what happened."

CHICHÓN IS LYING ON THE DUSTY MAT, SHAKING. VICTORIA rushes over to her.

"What happened? How did you get away from your uncle?"

"He won't be bothering me anymore," Chichón says, looking away.

CHAPTER FOURTEEN

It's after dark by the time Victoria and Chichón get to Andrés' hospital room.

Marko is sitting there. "Hey," he says, looking Chichón up and down, "since when are you a girl?"

"Since always. Can't you tell the difference, Botija?"

"No. You really fooled me."

"She really fooled me too," Victoria says.

"Should we call you Chicholina now?" Andrés asks.

"Wow." Marko is still shaking his head in disbelief. "And what's with the bandages?"

"My uncle beat me up again. But that's the last time he'll ever do it."

"We could have a competition to see who's in worse shape," Andrés says, trying to laugh.

Marko gets up. "I'm gonna get Gringo's bike back."

"The Captain will kill you!" Andrés says.

"No he won't. By the time he figures out who took it, I'll be gone." He waves the bus ticket to Concordia in the air. "I'd better get over there and get it before the boys dismantle it."

"You're crazy," Victoria protests. "Don't go!"

"It's my fault it got stolen. And I promised you I would fix things. And I will."

"We'll go with you," Victoria says.

"No. No way. It's my business, and I'll take care of it myself." Marko tips his cap and rushes out of the door.

"Marko has a good heart," Andrés says. "But he's a fool. You'd better try to stop him."

WHEN VICTORIA AND CHICHÓN REACH THE SIDEWALK, THEY find Marko is already getting into a taxi.

"I know where Botija's going," Chichón says, waving to a cab. "Let's follow him."

"Wait," Victoria stops her friend. "Are you sure? It'll be dangerous."

Chichón pulls her shirt up—a gun is stuck in the waistband of her jeans.

VICTORIA FOLLOWS CLOSE BEHIND CHICHÓN, MOVING slowly in the dim light of the crescent moon. They jump over a narrow ditch and sneak behind a large run-down shed. They creep up to a window with broken glass and peek in. Victoria feels Chichón's breath on her cheek.

It's filthy inside the shed. Tools, oil cans, cables, pulleys and broken bottles are strewn everywhere. Gringo's bike is next to the door, illuminated by a single light-bulb. Marko is lying on the ground looking up at the Captain. Marko's shirt is soaked with blood and his face is swollen.

"This is your last chance," the Captain says. "Where's the package?"

Silence.

"Tell me where it is." He presses the gun against Marko's head.

Chichón pulls out her gun, aims and fires at the Captain. He staggers backward, clutching his belly, and collapses.

"I got him," Chichón whispers. Victoria's knees buckle in relief.

The sound of another gunshot echoes through the shed.

"What's that?" Victoria gasps.

"He's shot Botija."

THE CAPTAIN'S EYES STARE BLANKLY AT THE CEILING. MARKO is writhing in pain on the oil-soaked floor.

"There's money I saved up and the bus ticket to Concordia in my backpack." Marko's voice is fading. He is struggling to speak. "Chichón, go to Montevideo and give the money to my mom for the flower shop. Here's her address." Marko reaches for something in his pocket.

Victoria puts her hand on his and helps him. It's an envelope. Inside are a letter and the photo of Marko as a little boy with his mother and his pup, Momo.

Chichón nods, unable to speak.

"Chiquilina," Marko says weakly, looking up at Victoria. "There's a lot more hidden in the oil can under the sink. Take it." Before he can say anything else, his body goes slack.

"Marko! Marko!" Victoria touches his face and shakes his shoulders.

"No time for that now," Chichón says, picking up Marko's backpack. "He's gone." She places the gun in Marko's hand. "You get the money. I'll start the motorcycle."

Victoria puts the letter and photo back in the envelope and tucks it in her pocket. A sob wracks her body. Then she wipes her eyes and stands up. The Captain is lying in a pool of blood in front of the sink. A revolting smell overwhelms her. She forces herself to step over his body and look for the money under the sink. It's inside the oil can, wrapped in neat bundles. Victoria stuffs them inside her shirt.

While Chichón revs up the motorcycle, Victoria goes back and kneels down next to Marko. She takes his yellow and black cap and puts it on her head.

The angels will watch over you. Dream, Botija, my friend.

She climbs on the bike behind Chichón, and they roar out of the garage. As they turn the corner, they hear sirens approach. Chichón swerves down a dirt road and cuts the engine.

A squad car, its lights flashing, careens past.

Then they speed back to the city.

Victoria hops off the motorcycle in front of Margarita's house. "Come in," Victoria says to Chichón. "You can sleep here tonight."

"No. The bus leaves early tomorrow morning. I'll stay at the café tonight. The guys will get the bike back to Gringo."

"Okay," says Victoria, sorry to say goodbye. *But it's the best thing for Chichón to do.*

They divide up the money under the street light and hug.

"Send me a letter and tell me everything."

"I will," Chichón says, before roaring off on the motorcycle.

The next day, as soon as she gets up, Victoria goes to the hospital. Andrés is awake and waiting impatiently for her.

"Come over here, muñeca," he says. "What happened? Did you stop Marko?"

"We got Gringo's motorcycle back," she says, then hesitates.

"What's wrong?" Andrés asks, pulling Victoria toward him with his good arm and drawing her close. "Is the Captain causing more trouble?"

Victoria shakes her head. "The Captain's dead."

"What! How?" Andrés exclaims.

"Chichón . . . she shot him. She was trying to save Marko, but she couldn't."

"What do you mean?"

Victoria's lips tremble and her face pales. "Marko is dead."

Andrés punches the mattress. "Mierda! He was going to go home today. His poor mother."

"I know." Victoria's eyes well up with tears, and she can no longer hold them back. *So much has happened in such a short time.*

Andrés brushes Victoria's hair away from her face and dries her tears.

The patient in the next bed turns up the radio, and tango music fills the room.

Things that have happened,
have not been in vain.
Life has shown me,
what I am like . . . both lost and found.

CHAPTER FIFTEEN

THREE MONTHS LATER, ANDRÉS IS SITTING ON A BENCH IN Urquiza Park next to the statue of the Indian girl with the arrow. He is holding a bouquet of jasmine.

"Mmmm, I love jasmine." Victoria kisses him, and he hands her the bouquet.

"How was school?" he asks.

"Great. I took a math test and did really well."

"Good for you, che."

"And I got a letter from Chichón today."

"What did she say?" Andrés asks.

"She's in Montevideo. Marko's mother opened a flower shop, and Chichón is working for her. She's really happy there."

"We should go visit them after the championships," Andrés says. "I'll buy the bus tickets."

"I'd love that," Victoria says.

"Come." He gets up, taking her by the arm. "Let's have a bite at Los Andes."

"Sure, I'd like to say hi to the guys there," Victoria says. As they walk, she adds, "I was thinking of going to Doña Frida's later."

"You've been going there a lot since Betina moved in," Andrés says.

"I like it there. I help Doña Frida, and I see the twins when Betina brings them for a visit."

Andrés smiles warmly. When they get close to the café, he puts his hands over Victoria's eyes.

"What are you doing?" she asks, puzzled.

"You'll see." He guides her inside and takes his hands away.

"SURPRISE!"

Betina, the twins and Bite'm, Margarita, Cacho, Beto, Moustache, Doña Frida and Gringo are there. A red banner above the bar reads:

HAPPY BIRTHDAY, VICTORIA!

Betina starts singing, and Beto joins in with his guitar. Moustache comes up to Andrés. "I saw your picture in the paper. I can't believe it. All the customers talk about you."

"Wait until the championships," Andrés jokes, walking over to Gringo who is sitting at the big table.

The twins play with Bite'm.

Cacho walks in, holding a chocolate cake with fifteen candles. "I baked it myself."

Betina sings "Happy Birthday" and everybody joins in. Victoria is so happy she doesn't know what to say. Everyone gathers around while she blows out the candles. She and Cacho slice up the cake and serve it.

"Che, Beti, thanks for the surprise party," Victoria says as she hands her cousin a plate.

"It was Andrés' idea. Listen, Doña Frida wants to talk to you. Her daughter is getting married soon and will be moving to her own place."

"She won't be needing her room anymore," Doña Frida says. "I thought you might want to take it."

Victoria's face lights up, and then she shakes her head at Doña Frida. "I think I should stay where I am—it doesn't cost me anything. I need to save my money for the twins."

"But my daughter never paid rent," Doña Frida says, smiling. "If you help Marilén with the chores after school, you'll be doing me a big favour."

"And I can give your bed to another girl," Margarita says, joining in.

Victoria looks back and forth between the two women, overwhelmed.

Doña Frida places a kind hand on Victoria's shoulder. "You'll have your own room at my place, and you'll be able to have the twins overnight sometimes. I know that's important to you."

Victoria wipes away her tears. "Thank you! Thank you, Doña Frida!"

She hugs her tightly. "And thank you too, Doña Margarita!" She hugs her as well, choking back a sob.

A little later, Victoria walks over to Andrés who is trying to play Beto's guitar. "Thank you so much for my party. Everything's just perfect." She bends down and gives him a kiss.

"You're the one who's perfect."

Mamá, you were right. Everything will be okay.

Softly, Victoria sings.

> *A new road is beginning,*
> *where a dream waits to blossom for you,*
> *a day will dawn, bringing your new destiny*
> *and the nights of yesterday*
> *will become the shadows*
> *of today.*

GLOSSARY

amico:
  friend in Italian

bellezza:
  beauty in Italian

benteveo:
  kiskadee, bird

bicho feo:
  ugly bug (it's also the
  nickname for Benteveo
  derived from its birdcall)

boludo:
  dumb, slang in Argentina

Bomba Tucumana:
  the artistic name of an
  Argentine cumbia singer

Bostero:
  nickname for the Boca
  Juniors soccer team's fans

botija:
  kid, slang in Uruguay

camalote:
  water hyacinth

candombero:
  one who dances
  candombe, popular Afro-
  Uruguayan dance

chau:
  bye

che:
  you, slang in Argentina

chichón:
  bump

chiquilina:
  girl, slang in Uruguay

choripán:
  sandwich with chorizo (a
  sausage)

cogote:
  vulgar for neck

Come vai?:
  How are you? (in Italian)

cosita:
  little thing

cumbia:
  popular Latin American
  music

espinillo:
  gorse tree

estúpido:
  stupid

fuera:
  out

hijo de puta:
  son of a bitch

idiota:
  idiot

Jesús María:
  Jesus Mary

linda:
  nice

mamá:
  mom

mamita:
  little mom, endearment
  for mother

mate:
  A very popular drink
  (tea-like) in Argentina
  and Uruguay. It's served
  in a cup made of squash
  with a metal straw.

mate cocido:
  A very popular drink
  (tea-like) in Argentina.
  It's served in a cup.

mate cosido:
  scarred or sewn forehead,
  slang in Argentina

m'hija:
short for 'my daughter',
slang in South America

mi amor:
my love

mierda:
shit

muñeca:
doll

palo borracho:
tropical tree

peatonal:
pedestrian street

pelotudo:
dumb

pendeja/o:
little boy, derogatory,
slang in Argentina

piojito:
little louse

princesa:
princess

ragazza:
girl in Italian

señorita:
miss

siesta:
nap

surubí:
river fish in South
America

ta:
okay, slang in Uruguay

tía:
aunt

vo:
you, slang in Uruguay

SONGS

Duerme mi niña – Sleep My Girl
    by Víctor Prestipino and Mario Canaro (fragment)

Cafetín de Buenos Aires – Little Café from Buenos Aires
    by Enrique Discépolo y Mariano Mores (fragment)

La próxima puerta – The Next Door
    by Norberto Rizzi y Saúl Cosentino (fragment)

Te has comprado un automóvil – You'd Bought a Automobile
    by César Garrigós and Antonio Tanturi (fragment)

El firulete – The Twirl
    by Rodolfo Taboada and Mariano Mores (fragment)

En esta tarde gris – In This Gray Afternoon
    by José M. Contursi and M. Mores (fragment)

Comprale un choripán – Buy Her A Chorizo Sandwich
    by Pocho La Pantera (fragment)

Mirá qué negro que soy – Look at How Vulgar I Am
    by Supermerk-2 (fragment)

Tres amigos – Three Friends
    by Enrique Cadícamo (fragment)

Milonga por tantas cosas – Milonga for So Many Things
    by Amanda Velazco and Carmen Guzmán (fragment)

BIOS

The author, SILVANA GOLDEMBERG, *was born and raised in Argentina. She has been published in Spanish and English throughout the Americas. She now lives in Richmond, BC with her husband and two daughters.*

The translator, EMILIE TERESA SMITH, *is an Argentine-born writer and theologian. She has published several books for children, including* Viva Zapata! *for Tradewind Books. She is an Anglican priest working in the Diocese of New Westminster, BC.*